THE COLD HAND OF DEATH

OTHER TEAM REAPER THRILLERS

THE COLD HAND OF DEATH

A TEAM REAPER THRILLER
BOOK 17

BRENT TOWNS

ROUGH
EDGES
PRESS

AUTHOR'S NOTE

The Cold Hand of Death is the first time we see the appearance of ODIN, Global's elite extraction team. Led by former SBS commander, Ian Groves, ODIN take on tough jobs with their experienced operators—Helen Smith, Rose Holden, Paul Cross, and Evan 'Chuck' Norris. No job is too tough, as proved within the pages that follow.

Who knows, they might even pop up somewhere else in the future...

When I first started this book, a little over 12 months ago, I had no idea what kind of roadblocks it was going to throw at me. I thought it would just be straight forward like the rest. But no, things changed, the story changed, and it became like my nemesis. So, I stepped away and came back every time I could get it straightened out in my head.

It soon became clear that the mission was going to be a lot bigger than Team Reaper could handle, hence the appearance of ODIN, and Chief Borden Hunt.

But one thing in the story has remained constant—the action that the series readers are used to.

I hope you enjoy the ride.

Brent Towns
1/11/2022

For Steve Lepper, who answered the hard questions as only a diehard reader could.

THE COLD HAND OF DEATH

BEFORE...

"WHAT IS IT?" Edison asked in a less than hospitable tone.

The voice coming through the speaker of the phone said, "We've got a problem."

Edison listened quietly to the news, then grunted. "Get everything we have on it." He disconnected the call. Picking up another encrypted cell, he dialed a new number.

On the other end, President Richard Nelson said, "This better be good news."

"Not hardly. Kane got his sister out of the facility. Whoever was with him killed the security team before they left."

"Damn it, Brett. You were supposed to fix this. Where is he now?"

"We don't know."

"Shit. Put the bounty on his head. I want him found. Make it thirty million."

Edison's heart quickened with excitement. This was more like it. "Dead or alive, sir?"

"It won't make a difference, will it? Not with that amount of money involved."

"Yes, sir, Mister President."

———

TWO HOURS LATER IN THE SKY OVER THE ATLANTIC

One of the flight crew in the Globemaster walked toward Cara, a computer tablet with some earbuds in his hands. He held it out to her. "You need to see this."

She nodded her thanks and took the proffered tech, placing the earbuds into her ears as she tapped the screen. What she saw was a press conference being held by Brett Edison.

"*...need to be on the lookout for these two people.*" The screen changed and showed a picture of Kane and his sister Melanie.

"*They are extremely dangerous and should be treated as such. They are responsible for the murders of several government officials and under no circumstances should they be approached. Instead, we urge anyone who sees them to inform the authorities right away. I reiterate, they are extremely dangerous, and we believe the pair are working for a foreign government. Therefore, I have been instructed by the president to issue a reward for their capture or information leading to their capture. That reward will be thirty million dollars.*"

Cara was stunned. "Oh, Reaper, what have you gotten yourself into?"

PART ONE

LET THE DYING BEGIN

CHAPTER 1

SHENANDOAH NATIONAL PARK, VIRGINIA

JOHN "REAPER" Kane halted and helped his sister Melanie sit on a damp log to catch her breath. She was tiring fast, and he knew she couldn't go on much longer. He looked her over and asked, "How are you feeling?"

She looked up at him with tired brown eyes. Her dark hair hung down her back in long strands made stringy by the light rain filtering through the forest canopy. "I'm exhausted."

Kane lowered his six-foot-four frame down beside her, laying the Heckler and Koch 416 on the log within easy reach. He put an arm around her. "Just hang in there a little longer, Mel, and I'll get you out of here."

"Who were those men, John?" she asked him. "Why did they keep me locked up in that room?"

The former Recon Marine stared at her. "He—the man responsible—is after me."

"But why?"

"My team and I are thorns in his side. He had us

driven out of the US, and then he took you to get to me. Only he messed up by thinking it would be easy."

"Are you still in the Marines?"

"Didn't the doctor tell you?"

She shook her head. "He only mentioned some things."

Kane nodded. "No, I'm not in the Marines anymore. I was part of a special team that worked for the government. Things happened, and I was forced to leave."

Alarm showed on her face. She touched his arm. "What if they catch you?"

"They won't," he assured her.

"What are we going to do?"

"We have to get far away from here."

Kane stood up and took off his body armor, along with his ballistic helmet and night-vision goggles. He hid everything behind the log, including the carbine. The only things he kept were the SIG Sauer P226 handgun and the spare magazines.

"What are you doing?" Melanie asked.

"I need to ditch all this stuff before we go on. I would kind of stand out if I kept it, don't you think?"

She nodded, her gaze going to the bloody sleeve of his shirt. "Let me take a look at that wound."

Kane contemplated saying no, but a few extra minutes wouldn't hurt. He took off his shirt and placed it beside him. Melanie said, "Turn around."

"What?"

"Turn around. I want to look at your back."

He did as she asked. She reached out with a trembling hand to touch the Grim Reaper tattoo from which Kane took his handle. Her fingers traced it lightly, sending a weird sensation through Kane's nerve endings below the skin. After a minute or so, Melanie said in a soft voice, "It *is* you."

He turned back and saw the tears in her eyes. He scooped her up in his arms and pulled her close. "Of course it's me, Mel. Of course it's me."

"I-I'm sorry. I had to be sure."

"It's—" He stopped suddenly.

Melanie felt him tense. "What is it?" she whispered into his ear.

"I'm not sure." His hand slid down to the P226 tucked in his belt. "When I move, get down behind the log as fast as you can."

"John, I'm scared."

"Don't be. I've got you."

———

SOMEWHERE OVER THE ATLANTIC

"Ladies and gents, just to let you know we're being diverted," the voice from the cockpit came over the intercom filling Cara's headset.

She looked to the left and right of herself. All eyes were on her, faces wearing confused expressions. She said into the boom mic, "Roger that. What is our destination?"

"Venezuela, ma'am."

Another glance at the others told her all she needed to know. Their faces showed open disappointment with the altered situation. Like herself, they'd all been hoping to return to pick up Kane. It seemed that wasn't going to happen. She needed to show her leadership now more than ever. "Roger that. Venezuela it is."

She felt the Globemaster change course as one wing dipped and the other rose. Her mind wandered to Kane, trying to process what might be happening on the ground. She leaned back and removed the headset. Ran a hand through her short dark hair and let out a long sigh.

She felt a presence beside her and opened her eyes to see the bearded Raymond "Knocker" Jensen, the former SAS operator sitting there. "What do you make of it?"

"I don't know. We'll find out when we get there."

"For a moment I thought they were going to send us back."

"So did I."

———

SHENANDOAH NATIONAL PARK, VIRGINIA

Kane slipped a fresh magazine into his P226 and stared down at the man near his feet. Two more lay in the brush, another by a rock off to his left. He turned to see Melanie crouched shivering behind the log she'd been sitting on only moments before.

The shooters had come out of the dense undergrowth with the intention of killing them both. And they were good, but Kane was better. Now they lay dead.

"Wait there, Mel," Kane ordered his sister. "I'll be right back."

"John, wait," she whispered urgently. "What if there are more of them? Don't leave me."

"You'll be fine. I won't be far away."

Kane disappeared into the damp undergrowth. To Melanie it seemed to envelop him, swallow him up. Her breath caught in her throat and her chest constricted. Meanwhile, Kane started to work his way around in a large arc, trying to cut any sign that there might be more out there.

At first he found nothing, then a single boot print. He recognized it immediately. He'd seen the same print many times before. USMC Danner RAT boots. There was still someone out there in the brush. And he'd left Melanie on her own.

He moved silently back through the undergrowth toward where he'd left his sister, the wet foliage sweeping against his clothing leaving visible tracks. A hint of anxiousness started to filter into his normally calm interior and his pace quickened.

But even as he pushed through the last green wall in front of him, Kane knew he was too late. Even though his P226 was raised.

"Put it down," the man snarled at Kane. He had his own handgun pointed at Melanie's head. Melanie looked scared. She'd been through so much in such a short period of time.

"Let her go," Kane said in a calm voice. "It's me you want."

"I told you to put your gun down," the man hissed again.

Kane looked at his sister. "Are you all right?"

"No."

"It's OK. I've got this. Trust me."

"Please, John—"

"Hey!" the man shouted, causing Melanie to flinch. "What the fuck did I—"

The P226 in Kane's hand bucked, and the man's head snapped back, a hole in his forehead. At the same time Melanie gave a yelp of fear and then the man fell to the ground beside her.

Kane hurried forward and wrapped his arms around her. Melanie's shoulders trembled as emotion overcame her. Kane pulled her closer and kissed her on the cheek.

"It's OK, Mel. It's OK."

———

TEAM REAPER HQ, HEREFORD, ENGLAND

Former general, Mary Thurston was barking orders to her people at the same time the Globemaster was turning around. Her long dark hair was tied in a pony-tail which hung down her back and swung left and right as she strode purposefully across the operations room. "Luis, make sure that everything we need gets aboard that plane. I don't want to be halfway across the Atlantic and find out that we've not got something."

"Running check lists as we speak, Mary," former DEA agent Luis Ferrero replied. Late forties, solid build with graying hair, he was the man who had formed the team in the beginning.

"Great." She turned to Swift. "How solid is this intel, Slick?"

The Team's computer tech turned to face her. His red hair was longer than usual and hung down to his collar. The thirty-something computer whiz nodded and said, "Very solid, ma'am."

"Roger that. And get a damned haircut. You look like a hippie from Woodstock."

"Yes, ma'am."

Her next target was the commander of Bravo Team. Brooke Reynolds had long dark hair like her commander, had an athletic build, and was their UAV pilot. "Brooke, do we have a UAV nailed down yet?"

"Yes, ma'am, the guy at Global has sorted it for me on short notice. I'm really becoming fond of this place."

"Good. Teller, where are you?"

"Here, ma'am."

Reynolds's number two seat appeared behind her. Thurston stared at him. "Do you have everything you need?"

"And then some, ma'am." He nodded and smiled as he spoke.

"General," called a heavily accented voice from across the room.

She turned to see Carlos Arenas, the former Mexican Special Forces commander waving at her. "What is it, Carlos?"

"We're having trouble with the armorer again."

"Asshole. Tell him that if he doesn't give you what you want, I'll come over there and feed him his fucking balls."

"Yes, ma'am."

"Trouble, Mary?" asked a deep voice.

She turned and saw Hank Jones, now the commander of Global, standing there. "No, sir, just some organizational issues."

"I'm sure you'll handle it all with your usual aplomb."

"Yes, sir."

"Any news on Kane?"

"No, sir. All we know is that he's in the wind. I have to trust he knows what he's doing because we've got a mission we have to complete."

Jones nodded. He was a big man who closely resembled the general who had led the coalition forces in the First Gulf War, Norman Schwarzkopf Jr. He was also former special forces who ran recon "About that, Mary, how sure are you of your intel?"

"Slick says it's good, sir. I trust his judgement."

"Are you sure this is the way to go?"

Thurston stiffened. "Are you doubting *my* judgement, sir?"

Jones shook his head. "No, Mary. I just want to make sure that all is in order."

"We have solid intel that Edison has a shipment of arms coming ashore in La Guaira. We have container numbers, times, even the ship that it's coming off."

"Where did this intel come from?"

Thurston looked around. "Slick, where are you?"

He seemed to appear from nowhere. "Ma'am?"

"The general is concerned about your intel."

Swift looked at Jones. "Sir?"

"Where did it come from?"

"I did a deep search on the web and found the site where his customers place their orders. More digging and I was able to find that he has a shipment arriving in La Guaira two days from now. It's worth fifty million."

"What does it consist of?"

"Assault rifles, rocket launchers, ammunition,

grenades. It's nothing compared to the other one I found."

Jones frowned. "What other one?"

"The one consisting of assault rifles and ammunition, rocket launchers, claymores, handguns, sniper rifles, a Predator UAV, AK-74s, heavy caliber machine guns. I think I saw something about a tank as well."

Jones's eyebrows shot up. "A fucking tank?"

"Yes, sir. It seems Edison is well connected across the globe."

"How much?"

"Many millions. Hundreds of millions at least."

"Where?" Jones asked, his jaw set firm at the news.

"I'm not sure, sir. The delivery place doesn't appear until the shipment is ready, apparently." Swift shrugged. "Take your pick of any country that is self-imploding at the minute. My guess would be somewhere in Africa."

"And all of this money is going into Nelson's reelection campaign, right?"

"Yes, sir."

"Why?" Jones demanded.

"We don't know, sir. Whatever the reason, it must be good. We all got too close to it, and we all know how that ended."

Jones nodded. "All right, let's dry up the well. Put Edison out of business."

"That's what we aim to do," Thurston replied with a sly smile.

———

ARLINGTON NATIONAL CEMETERY, ARLINGTON,
VIRGINIA— THE FOLLOWING DAY

Vice President Jack Reed knelt next to the headstone, head bowed, resting his right hand on top of its smooth, cold surface. His lips moved in silent prayer, his eyes shut tight. His Secret Service detail leader stood a few meters away to give his boss privacy in this solemn moment. The journey to Arlington was a regular once a month event when Reed would visit his son's grave. Sam Reed had been killed twelve months before in Nigeria. He'd been leading a small Special Forces unit on a raid to rescue three missionaries who'd been held captive by rebels for six months.

The team had been inserted during the dead of night, traversed the terrain for a couple of kilometers before hitting the target.

No one was really sure what happened after that. Once the shooting started, everything seemed to go wrong. The intel was screwed, the hostages weren't there, and instead of being a handful of militia onsite, there were around fifty.

Of the six operators who'd inserted, two were wounded and Sam Reed was killed.

Today, the detail leader was Dan Harris. He was a solidly built man with ten years' experience working the White House. He turned his gaze to the six vehicles where the rest of his detail waited near the four black Suburbans and two black and whites from the PD. All his command looked to be switched on. Which was good for them. One thing he would never tolerate was a slack agent. That cost lives. That—

WHAP!

"What the fuck?"

Harris heard the VP grunt and saw him start to topple to his left. It took only a heartbeat for him to realize what had just occurred. "He's down! The—"

WHAP!

It felt as though the air had been hammered from Harris's lungs. He tried to breathe and at first nothing came. Then when it did he heard a hollow rasping sound. He looked down and saw the blood on his shirt where his coat had opened. It revealed a hole in the fabric where blood started to run freely, small bubbles indicating the escaping air.

Harris sank to his knees. He could hear his detail shouting to each other. Voices slowly faded as the surrounding darkness closed in on him.

———

LANGLEY, VIRGINIA

"What the fuck happened?" Alex Joseph demanded into the phone's handset.

"The details are still sketchy, sir. All we know right now is that the vice president was shot and killed while visiting his son's grave."

"What about his detail? What were they doing? Did they have their thumbs up their asses?"

"I know he was your friend, sir, and for that I'm sorry," the man on the other end said. "But I'm afraid I can't give you the answers you want because I don't have them."

"Well, get out there and fucking find them. This

place is going batshit crazy," he growled and slammed the receiver down. "Fuck!"

Joseph sat back and stared at the ceiling. Thoughts ran through his head at a million miles a minute. "Fuck it," he growled and reached for his phone. "Bring my car around. There's somewhere I need to go."

Joseph rose from his seat and hurried towards the door. He threw it open and strode purposefully through.

"Admiral," a young lady in a pants suit called to him.

"I'm not here, Celia. Do you see me?"

"No, sir."

"Then I'm definitely not fucking here."

"Yes, sir." She looked at the floor, not certain what she should do.

He hurried outside and climbed into the rear seat of the SUV which waited for him. In the front was a young man who turned and looked at Joseph and asked, "Where to, sir?"

"Anvil. I need to go and see the others. Something isn't right. Do you know where they are?"

"Yes, sir."

Then as they pulled away, the SUV disappeared in a large ball of orange flame as the bomb beneath it detonated with a savage fury.

———

WASHINGTON

"What the hell were you thinking?" President Richard Nelson seethed at Edison. "First the vice president and then the head of the CIA." He ran a hand through his graying hair in frustration.

The fifty-year-old director of national intelligence looked calm as he sat in the chair opposite. "That wasn't me, it was them. Besides, it had to be done. The old prick was starting to get in the way."

"But did it have to be done so fucking publicly?"

"Think of it as a warning."

Nelson stabbed a finger at him. "This is bullshit. Who do they think is running this country?"

"Do you want to be president next year or not?" Edison snapped.

"You know the answer to that. But the way things are it will be in title only. We all know who is running this show."

"Then don't make them angry. Remember, they came to us."

"They were supposed to stay in the shadows."

"With Joseph still alive it would never have happened. And don't worry, it will never be traced back to us. They are too good for that."

Nelson raised his eyebrows and gave Edison a disgruntled stare. "Really?"

Edison knew what he meant. "Things happen."

"Well make them unfucking happen. Where are we at?"

"Still no sign of Kane and his sister, and Joseph's cadre have gone to ground."

"What about Mary Thurston and her people?"

"We're still working on that. The good news is that the hotline is going crazy with people dialing in to claim the reward."

"How is that a good thing?"

"It means they're looking. Something will turn up."

"Make something happen."

"I could always bring in Forest."

For a moment, Nelson looked alarmed. "Are you kidding?"

"It has been suggested that I do it."

"Christ."

"Well, they handed Bear Travis's ass to him on a plate. Maybe we need to bring in the heavy hitters. If anyone can find Kane, it's him and his team."

"And leave a trail of bodies across the country while they're doing it," Nelson pointed out.

"All for a second term, Mister President."

"All for them."

"There's that, too."

"Do they think I'm a fucking puppet?"

"Do you want me to answer that?"

"Fine. But you oversee him."

Edison went quiet.

"What is it?" Nelson asked.

"I'm going to be out of the country for a week or so."

"What do you mean?"

"I'm going to be securing funds."

"Selling arms you mean," Nelson snapped.

"Orders. I have a sale in Venezuela and a much larger one in Africa. Then I'll be back. If all goes well it will benefit the new government in more ways than one."

"Damnit, Brett—"

"Let me worry about everything, Richard. You just concentrate on talking up your next vice-president."

"How can I when he'll be out of the country? You're needed here to deal with *them*."

Once again there was more silence followed by sudden dread.

"What is it?"

"There has been a change. I won't be your VP anymore."

"Who—who will be?"

"Randall Coster."

Nelson's face paled. Coster was a senator from Texas, the unofficial leader of *Them* as Nelson referred to them. "And why am I just finding this out?"

"It's too late to go back now. You gave them an inch. Now you have to see it all the way through. Even if it burns down around your ears."

The door opened and a tall, broad-shouldered man walked in.

Edison looked at Nelson and said, "I'm sure you'll work something out."

Randall Coster straightened, stared at the president, and growled, "Right, Nelson, let's get this fucking shit fixed."

———

WEST VIRGINIA

The four men watched the report for a fourteenth time in stunned silence. Not one of them could believe what they were seeing yet they all knew it was true.

"Fucking sons of bitches," Former Master Chief Grady Ruggles snarled in his deep growl. The tough one-time BUDs instructor glanced at the man beside him.

Former SEAL chief Borden Hunt stared stoically at

the television. The four of them had been holed up in the country safehouse ever since they had helped Kane and his sister get away.

"They'll come after us next," a voice said from the sofa.

Rucker turned his head to look at the wounded SEAL. "Let them come, Striker."

Hunt shook his head. "No. We need to get out. Where's the sat phone?"

"On the table," Ruggles replied.

Hunt walked to the coffee table in the center of the room and picked up the phone, a voice he knew well answering his call. "Is that you, Scimitar?"

"Yes, sir. I need your help. Have you heard about the admiral?"

"I did. You want out?"

"Yes, sir."

"Make for point Echo, son, and I'll get you out."

"There will be four of us, General," Hunt informed Jones.

"It's all good, Bord. Just be at Echo in two days."

"Thank you, sir."

"One more thing. Is there any sign of our lost souls?"

"Not as yet, sir."

"All right. Echo. Two days."

The call disconnected. Hunt turned to the others. "Striker, can you move?"

"I can fucking run if I need to."

"Fine. Everybody gear up, we've got territory to cover."

———

SOMEWHERE IN MEXICO

Trent Forest peered through the binoculars at the pissant village nestled below the ridgeline. A fly buzzed around his ear but the forty-year-old mercenary with the shaved head ignored it, intent on his target below.

"I don't see shit," said a man with a heavy British accent who lay beside him.

"He's there all right, Badger," Forest replied. "So are the rest of his fucking cock suckers."

Lester "Badger" Miller looked sideways at his boss and said, "If you say so."

"I do. Get everyone ready, we're going down there."

"Roger that."

Their target was one Manuel Ortiz. Drug runner and people smuggler. The village was where he and his coyotes called home. He was wanted for the murder of a Texas oil tycoon's wife twelve months ago. Forest didn't know the details, nor did he care. The money was good, and he and his people would earn it. One thing they did was get the job done, no matter what.

He slid back from the crest of the ridge and stood up. Turning, he looked at his people as they readied themselves.

Bill Knowles, 34, former New York cop, kicked off the force for being overly aggressive with a suspect. His justification was that the man had been resisting arrest, but the board of inquiry didn't see that a broken arm, three busted ribs, a fractured jaw, and thirty stitches in the face was appropriate force.

Next to him, checking his equipment, was Virgil Zane. He was the team's comms specialist. The 28-

year-old former Marine had been kicked out for banging a general's wife.

That left Crypto Graph. No one remembered his first name; he'd always just been Crypto. Mid-twenties, computer tech-come-door kicker with a penchant for doing drugs. However, threatened with pain of death from Forest should he ever be caught with them in the field, Crypto chose not to be left out there with a bullet in his head.

The team was about to move when Zane said, "Got a message coming in over the secure wire."

He turned the Toughbook around so that Forest could see. The mercenary frowned. "Fucking where?"

Zane turned it back and saw why Forest had grown impatient. The computer was still linked to the satellite. He hit a button and turned it back. "There."

Forest looked at the message and shook his head. "When it rains, it pours. All right, let's get this job done. We've got another one waiting for us."

––––––––

The moans of the dying could be heard amongst the screams of the desperate. Forest changed out the spent magazine of his Heckler and Koch G36 and looked around him. The bodies were everywhere. Except for the one they wanted.

"I've got something over here, Tree," Knowles said over the comms. "Second to last house on the right."

"On my way," replied Forest as he turned on his heel and started to stride purposefully towards the end of the street.

A screech to his right drew his attention in time to

see a woman, dress torn, torso exposed, running towards him with what looked to be a machete. Almost casually he brought his weapon around and shot her in her naked chest.

Even though her legs stopped running her momentum carried her forward and she fell face down on the street.

When Forest reached the target building he found Knowles and Miller waiting for him. "What is it?"

"We've got a tunnel," Knowles told him.

"Shit. Why does there always have to be a fucking tunnel?" Forest growled. "Show me."

They went inside the house. As they passed through the doorway the mercenary saw Knowles step high. He looked down and saw the tripwire. "What's it hooked to?"

"A grenade," Miller said.

Taking care, Forest stepped high to clear it. Once inside he followed Knowles into the kitchen where the tunnel was exposed. "It was beneath the table."

"Have you been down there?"

"No. Thought you'd like to be the first and claim all of the glory for yourself."

Forest shook his head. "Fuck off."

Then Forest did something which surprised his men. He took a grenade from his webbing, removed the pin, and threw it down the hole.

"Motherfucker," Miller gasped and started running.

All three had just cleared the house and thrown themselves to the ground when the secondary explosions rocked the village. The first acted as the trigger for whatever Ortiz had down there.

Explosions quaked the landscape in an undulating

line from the rear of the house, running out into the desert. Ten of them.

Once the explosions had stopped, the three men climbed to their feet. Knowles said, "That was fucking smart."

Forest grinned the way a drunken teenager would and said, "Wasn't it?"

They followed the line of the blasts. What had once been a shallow tunnel was now a collapsed trench in the parched landscape. When they reached the end where the mouth had been, exiting in a dry wash, they found their target. The blast had thrown him the last few feet clear of the tunnel mouth and ripped his right leg off in the process.

"Looks like he won't be running to the pub anytime soon," Miller said with a chuckle.

Forest raised his weapon and shot the target twice, then ordered, "Get a picture and send it to the customer. We've got somewhere else to be."

CHAPTER 2

SHENANDOAH VALLEY, VIRGINIA

KANE CAME in from outside the cabin and found Melanie sleeping on the cot. He stood over her, listening to her breathing. He still couldn't believe that she was here.

However, it was time for them to move. They couldn't stay there forever. The other thing he needed to do was make contact with someone from Hereford, if not, Thurston.

He hated to do it, but...

"Mel, wake up."

She didn't move.

"Mel, it's time to go."

"Hmm?" An eye cracked open. "John?"

"Yes, it's me. We need to leave. It's getting dark."

She sat up and rubbed at her eyes. "Already?"

"Afraid so."

"What's the plan?" she asked her brother.

"I need to make a call. But first, I have to find a phone."

Melanie got to her feet. "Alright, let's go."

———

Two hours later, under a silvery moon, came their first break. A roadside bar. There were a handful of vehicles in the parking lot which could prove to be beneficial. But first they needed a cell.

"Wait out here while I go inside," Kane said.

Melanie put her hand on his arm. "Wait. Someone might recognize you."

He nodded. "More than likely but I need to find out what's happening and get a phone."

"Can't we wait for someone to come out?"

"We could be waiting a long time."

She nodded. "All right."

Kane turned from her and headed inside. It wasn't his best idea by a long shot, but he wasn't prepared to sit around and wait.

As soon as the door squeaked its protest at being opened, nearly every head within hearing distance turned to look. Which was almost everyone in the bar. Melanie had been right. It was a bad idea.

He paused and the long-haired young woman behind the bar said, "We use it to scare the strangers away."

Kane smiled. "It almost worked."

"What'll it be?"

"Beer."

She grabbed him a bottle and placed it on the bar in

front of him. He paid for it, and she walked off, leaving Kane to case the room.

Behind the bar the television was on running through a news cycle. Suddenly a picture of Alex Joseph appeared on the screen with headlines screaming at him that the former admiral had been killed in an explosion.

Kane felt like he'd been punched in the stomach. The young woman behind the bar saw him looking at the television and said, "Terrible thing. Two in as many days."

"What do you mean?"

"The vice president was killed as well. They're blaming Venezuelan rebels. They released it this afternoon."

Kane stared at the screen. Venezuelan rebels...bullshit. It was like the Cabal all over again. He looked around the room. He needed access to a phone and to get the hell out.

Suddenly the picture on the television changed and the screen went to the game. It looked like the Broncos were playing someone at home. Not that Kane was interested. He was more of a baseball fan. But there were plenty in the bar that were, and a lot of eyes went to the screen on the far wall which showed the same as the one behind the bar.

Kane took a pull on his beer and placed it on the bar. Near him, a man had his eyes glued to the big screen. On the bar he had some loose change and his cell. Just the thing that Kane needed.

He waited patiently. As he looked around the room, he could see the odd person looking in his direction.

The door opened and a large man walked in. He

almost looked out of place. The door alarm screeched as he entered, making most look in his direction before going back to the game.

However, when the big man saw Kane, he paused slightly. It wasn't much, just enough to put the Team Reaper man on edge. He needed to get out. He was too exposed.

Forgetting the cell, he started towards the door.

The big man stepped in front of him. Kane was by no means small, but this guy was bigger. He gave Kane a wolfish grin and said in a low voice, "Where do you think you're going?"

"Out the door."

"Got someone who wants to meet you."

"It'll have to wait."

The man shook his head. "I don't think so. We got your sister."

Blood boiled.

Kane still had his handgun but hesitated to use it inside the bar. Too many innocents around. Instead he moved with sudden speed and grabbed the big man's coat lapels and dragged him close. He brought his right knee up into the man's groin, crippling him almost immediately.

With a painful grunt, the man sank slowly to his knees. Kane, however, wasn't done with him. As the room erupted suddenly at a kicked goal on the screen, the noise was sufficient to cover the sound of the man's neck breaking.

When the girl behind the counter looked around, Kane was gone, along with the cell that had been sitting on the bar.

Although it had become colder outside Kane ignored it. The parking lot gravel crunched noisily under his feet as he walked cautiously out into the open. About halfway across the lot he was surprised at the appearance of a familiar face.

Bear Travis looked angrier than usual. "Going somewhere, Kane?"

The man they call Reaper looked around the parking lot for Melanie but couldn't see her. "That depends."

"$30 million is a lot of money. Thought I might cash in on the payday."

Kane nodded. "Well, you won't have to split it in half."

Travis's eyes narrowed. "This is where it ends, asshole."

"You get one chance to walk away, Travis. After that, there's nothing for you, only death."

"Yeah, and the death will be yours."

The man's hand moved with a blur, coming up with a fist full of black Glock. Kane had been expecting no less and reciprocated, his own handgun putting in an appearance, the resulting showdown resembling a scene from a 1950s western.

Shots rang out and the bounty hunter/killer dropped to the hard ground of the parking lot. Almost immediately Melanie appeared. He looked at her, could see the fear on her face. "Come on," he said. "We have to get out of here."

"Sir, I can't reach the team," Kane said into the cell.

"They're running a mission, Reaper," Hank Jones replied. "Damn, it's good to hear your voice, son. How are things?"

"I need out."

"Point Echo, two days."

"Yes, sir. Is it true? About the admiral."

"Afraid so, son."

"What can I do, sir?"

"You can get your ass to the RV, son," Jones growled. "No cowboy shit this time around. There's something bigger at play here."

"The Cabal?" Kane asked.

"No, something else."

"Roger that."

The call disconnected.

"Is everything all right?" Melanie asked, her visage revealing concern for her brother.

"I'm not sure."

––––––––

LA GUAIRA, VENEZUELA

The team had been on the ground in La Guaira for a couple of hours; unlike the Bravo element who were flying to Georgetown in Guyana. A short, stocky MI6 officer named Watson had picked them up at an airfield not marked on any maps. Each team member was dressed in civilian clothing, carrying weapons only available in Venezuela itself. This mission was off the books, and no one was to know that they were there. If the Venezuelan government got even a whiff of their presence, there'd be hell pay and they'd all probably wind up in prison, pending execution.

Watson had delivered the team to an abandoned trucking company yard. That was where they set up the few resources they had and waited for dark so Cara and Brick could go out and recon the waterfront.

"The best intel we have is that the ship will be arriving two days from now," Watson informed them.

Cara looked at him. "That's what our tech tells us as well. I thought I might go and run recon down there tonight. Have a look around, see what we can expect when the ship arrives."

"I know what you can expect," Watson replied. "There will be guns everywhere watching every move."

"Then it's a good thing we'll be prepared. Do you have a vehicle we can take?"

"There's an old Land Rover out the rear that should get you there and back."

So for the next two hours the team went over their equipment, checking and rechecking, familiarizing themselves. The one thing they didn't want to do was go into battle with weapons and equipment they knew nothing about. They had to trust in their confidence with the weapons. And all credit to the British. They had supplied them some decent gear.

Each operator was provided with an FN FNC assault rifle as well as Glock 17s. "Strip them down. Put them back together, get to know them inside out," Cara ordered them. "When we go into battle, I don't want anybody's weapon jamming up."

"My weapon has been jammed up for a long time," Knocker said with a broad grin.

"Maybe you should watch where you put it," Cara shot back at him.

"Or maybe he should stop following Axe around and screwing the silly cows he leaves behind," Brick added.'

"Who screws cows?" Axe asked.

Brick shot Knocker a grin.

"Oh, I get it," Axe growled. "It's that fucking English again."

"Speaking of cows," Knocker said. "What is—"

"Fuck off, nothing."

"I haven't even asked my question."

"Good."

"Are you single again?"

"Define single."

Knocker turned his gaze on Cara. She shook her head. "Frigging hopeless."

The Brit nodded. "And another lovely lass makes a last-minute escape."

"Fuck off."

They all laughed.

"Am I missing something?" Watson asked.

"Long story," Knocker replied. "I'll tell you over a couple of beers when we have time."

The MI6 man frowned. "I'll look forward to it. I think."

"I wonder who his next tattoo will be?" Brick said.

"Ha, ha, very fucking funny," Axe growled.

"I bet it's Daisy," Knocker said.

"Who the fuck is Daisy?" Axe asked as he started to strip his weapon.

"Moo," the Brit said, and they all laughed once more.

"I had to ask," Axe moaned. "Shit."

CHAPTER 3

THE UNITED STATES

THERE WAS STILL one day to go until the rendezvous time at Echo. Kane had relieved Bear Travis of the keys to his SUV (as he wouldn't be needing it) and they had covered some good territory. They were running well and would make the Echo point ahead of schedule. Even if it wasn't by much.

Seriously concerned about Melanie's wellbeing, Kane decided to take a chance on The Sundowner, a backwoods motel in a small town called Cullen. Being so early in her recovery, he figured she would appreciate a rest for a couple of hours, and them still make the RV.

The rat-faced desk clerk looked suspiciously at Kane. The one thing the dated reception area had going for it was that it was poorly lighted, and it was already dark. He said, "That'll be sixty dollars. Each."

"Bit steep, isn't it?"

"Take it or leave it. Who are you going to complain to?"

Right then and there, Kane should have realized that he was in trouble. Maybe he underestimated the man standing behind the counter, but at that point he, like Melanie, was tired and he just wanted a bed. He handed over the money and took the key.

Outside the door to their room, the bare light globe was being divebombed by a multitude of bugs, and Kane waved them away as he waded through them to insert the key. The dingy room was much like the reception area. It was dimly lit, and everything was brown. Bedcovers, carpet, curtains. Everything. Melanie screwed her nose up as she looked around and said, "What a dump."

Kane nodded. "You can have the double bed. I'll take this single. We'll get some sleep and then we'll head out in the morning before daylight. Thirty or forty more miles, and we'll be there."

"What exactly is 'there,' John?"

"Echo is an old World War Two Air Force Base. It was shut down in 1956, but basically everything was left there. They just walked away."

"And this is where we have to go?"

"That's it.

She sat on the edge of the bed. "What then? How do we get out of here?"

"If I know the general, he'll have something lined up."

"I hope so. I never thought I would hear myself say this, but I really want to get out of this country."

"It's not the country, Mel. It's just certain people in it."

"Yes, the ones that are trying to kill us."

Kane shrugged. "You get used to it after a while."

"I don't think so." Her tone was soft and her face looked drawn and dejected.

"Have yourself a shower. You'll feel better afterwards."

"I would if I had some clean clothes," she replied, slapping her hand on her pants.

"I'm afraid I can't do much about that."

She flopped back onto the bed, lying there, staring at the ceiling. A few of the bugs from outside had managed to enter the room with them and were butting heads against the dim light. "Even if we get out of this, there's always going to be that hanging over our heads."

Kane stared at her. "Once we get to England, we'll be fine. After that, things have a way of sorting themselves out."

She looked thoughtful for a moment and then sat up hurriedly. "You mean you will sort them out. That's it, isn't it? You'll go and declare your own private little war, get yourself killed, and then I'll have no one."

"They have to be stopped, Mel. Besides, the general said there was more to it. Something's pulling all the strings behind the scenes. We need to find out what it is, and then we can stop it that way."

"I don't like it."

"Neither do I, but that's just how it works."

She stood up. "Fine. I'll go and have a shower."

———

Kane would later describe them as backwoods rednecks. They came out of the dark in three ancient and rusted out trucks. He heard their approach long before they pulled into the parking lot. Something to do with the lack of exhaust systems. Melanie was still in the shower.

He walked over to the curtain and pulled it back slightly in time to see twelve men climb from their vehicles. All were armed, some with guns, others with bats or lumps of wood. Kane shook his head. "I knew it."

He walked over to the single bed where he'd left his P226. He racked the slide, making sure a round was in the breech. Then he walked over to the bathroom door and called out, "I just have to go out for a minute. I'll be right back."

"Okay. Be careful."

Kane unlocked the door and stepped out onto the concrete walkway which ran the length of the motel. He was just in time to see the desk clerk hurrying across the parking lot. "What the fuck, Bubba?"

"Just shut up. We got this. There's money standing right there."

A quick mental calculation told Kane that six of them had weapons. Which wasn't great odds, but he'd faced worse. "Are you boys sure you want to do this?"

The one named Bubba said, "Are you him?"

"Who is him?"

"The one they're looking for on the news? The one they've got the bounty on? They say you're a traitor."

"You don't want to do this," Kane cautioned.

"Do you know what we do with traitors around here? We string them up. And since you is wanted dead or alive, that's probably a good thing to do to you."

Kane left his hand resting on the butt of the SIG in the back of his pants. "Before you do anything, answer this question. Which one of you wants to die first? Now I'm guessing that not one of you has ever taken a man's life. I've done it more times than I care to count. So when it comes to my life against your life, mine's going to win out every time. So again, who wants to die first?"

They gave each other nervous looks. Trying to find the courage to make the first move. The man named Bubba, took a step forward. "Shit, I'll—"

Kane's weapon came from behind his back and fired. The bullet hammered into the flesh of the man's left leg, throwing it out from beneath him. The redneck fell to the ground in a screaming heap. Blood pulsed from the wound.

The SIG in Kane's hand waved back and forth, covering the small group in front of him. "All right, then make your choice. Who's next?"

"Do you mind if we get in on this?" asked a familiar voice.

Out of the shadows stepped two men. Familiar faces, ones Kane was ever grateful to see. "Bord, Master Chief. Good to see you."

"Looks like you're having a little bit of trouble, Reaper," Hunt said. "Thought maybe we'd even up the odds a little."

"All help gratefully accepted. Although I did have it under control."

Ruggles stepped forward. "Any of you fucking pussies want to keep this dance going?"

The group of rednecks all took a step backward.

"Thought so. Pick your shit eating friend up and get the hell out of here."

They scrambled to do as the former master chief ordered. But there was one amongst them that Kane wasn't finished with. Stabbing his finger at the clerk, he growled, "You, come here."

"Me? You want me to come over there?"

"Trust me, asshole, you don't want *me* to come over *there*."

The young man took a few tentative steps forward —placing his hands on his hips in a false sense of bravado—until he was within Kane's reach. Suddenly Kane's fist shot out and clipped him under the chin. The clerk sat down hard, blinking, shaking his head. "What did you do that for?"

"Be thankful it wasn't a bullet. Now get out of here."

The young man jumped up and stumbled away, looking over his shoulder as he went.

Kane turned and looked at Hunt. "I'm sorry about the admiral, Bord."

"Me, too, Reaper. They got Anvil, too."

"Shit. I didn't know that. Where's Striker and Rucker?"

"We're not far away."

Kane turned and saw the other two SEALs materialize out of the darkness. He noted that Striker was limping. "You got a dog bite or something?"

The two special operators grinned. Striker said, "Or something."

"You guys want to take this inside?" Kane asked, indicating towards his room.

Hunt nodded. "Might be the best course of action, although we shouldn't hang around here for very long now."

"Just as soon as I get Mel organized, we can go."

"How is she, Reaper?" Ruggles asked.

"Scared. Confused. But she's holding up." He looked at Rucker. "Do you think you could take a look at her while we're preparing to leave?"

The combat medic nodded. "Yeah, I'll give her a quick once over. I'm sure she'll be fine."

"Thanks, doc."

When they entered the room, they found Melanie was out of the shower, but with a surprised look on her face. She looked at the group of strangers with her brother and became suddenly alarmed. "John—"

"It's all right. They're friends."

She looked unsure for a moment but then relaxed a little. Kane said, "We need to move again, Mel. All right?"

"All right."

"Rucker is just going to look you over. He's a medic. Just relax."

Rucker looked her over and then turned to Kane. "As far as I can tell, she's fine. But she does need rest."

"She can sleep in the SUV."

"I'll come with you," Rucker said.

"What about Striker?"

"He's not going to die."

"Fine, let's go."

———

Thirty minutes after Kane and the others left, three black SUVs swung into the lot and regurgitated their loads. Forest and Virgil Zane strode purposefully past the two police cruisers which had arrived on site twenty minutes earlier, and two deputies were inside the office questioning the clerk.

A fresh-faced young constable in a uniform looked at the two new arrivals and said, "Who are you?"

"Never you mind," Forest said simply before asking the clerk, "Where did they go?"

"Hey," the second deputy said interrupting. "He asked you a question."

Forest turned on him. "Are you going to keep pestering me while I try to talk?"

"Until I get answers," the deputy replied.

Forest glared at him briefly before making his decision. He pulled his concealed weapon and shot the deputy in the head.

The other young deputy was swift to react, but even so was too slow, for Zane executed him on the spot as well.

The clerk looked aghast at what he'd witnessed and could not hold his dignity, his bladder emptying on the tiled floor where he stood. His hands trembled, his lips quivered, and his legs turned to jelly. "P—please don't kill me. I didn't see anything. Honest."

"Where did they go?" Forest asked, repeating the question.

"Who?"

"The ones who were here."

Crypto Graph appeared in the doorway. "The FBI will be here shortly. You need to get what you want now."

Forest turned back to look at the clerk. "You've got exactly ten seconds to tell me where they went, or I'm going to put a bullet in your head."

"I overheard them talking when they left. They mentioned something about Echo. That's it. That's everything."

"Thank you," Forest said. And shot the young clerk in the head. "Check if there's any security cameras then disable and wipe them. Then let's get out of here."

"Are we headed there?" Crypto asked.

"No," Forest replied. "Let the Texans earn their money. We get paid either way."

———

POINT ECHO—THE FOLLOWING DAY

"We've got an hour until pickup," Hunt said to Kane.

They had reached Echo thirty minutes earlier and now they waited for extraction. The area where the old airfield used to be was flat and the buildings, even the old Quonset huts, were still in reasonably good shape.

The runways were virtually gone, reclaimed by nature over the intervening years. The flight tower was still upright, and it was here that Ruggles had set up his OP so he could see all 360 degrees of the old base.

Thunder rolled to the west and Kane turned his head. Steel-gray clouds with large curtains of rain suspended beneath them drove relentlessly across the landscape.

"I'll be glad to get out of here," Kane replied. "Just for Mel's sake."

"How is she doing?" Hunt asked, looking at Kane's sister sitting on a rusted steel chair beside an old milk crate they'd found outside a building.

"Better than I thought she would be. Even after all she's been through, she's as tough as they come. Takes after our grandfather."

"Tough old coot?"

"Vietnam War vet. SOG."

"Tough and with big balls."

"Inspired me to be what I am today."

"What are you going to do once we're out of here?" Hunt asked.

"Rejoin my team," Kane replied. "What about you?"

"See if Jones will give me a job. We've got nothing now."

Kane nodded. "Yeah, I know what that's like. Mind you, Global are a pretty tight unit. You could do worse. The only thing is family."

"I've got no one. Ruggles—well—no one would have him. I think Rucker still has his parents, and I'm not sure about Striker."

The humid air was split by a piercing whistle. They looked up at the tower and saw Ruggles pointing to the east. "We've got trouble," Hunt surmised.

He scooped up his Heckler & Koch 416 the team had kept after the raid on the facility where Melanie had been rescued. Kane nodded at it. "You got one of them for me?"

"Sorry."

He took out the P226 and checked it. "This'll have to do."

Kane motioned to Mel and they hurried inside one of the buildings and looked out through a glassless window frame. They were quickly joined by Rucker and a hobbling Striker. "What's the trouble?" asked Rucker.

"Not sure. The master chief saw something."

"With his eyesight it was probably a fly on the end of his nose," Striker growled.

"I heard that, smartass," Ruggles said as he joined them. "We've got incoming hostiles through the brush at our twelve as we stand. I figure maybe twenty tangos. More than—"

Ruggles failed to finish his sentence as a bullet smashed into the side of his head.

"Shit!" Hunt exclaimed. "Contact right!"

The shock of seeing their friend killed before their eyes lasted only moments before their training kicked in. They all scattered for cover, Kane taking the dead master chief's 416 as he went.

"Did you see where it came from?" Kane shouted.

"Tree line," Striker shouted back from behind a concrete barrier where he'd managed to lurch, dragging a panicked Mel with him.

"Has to be a sniper," Hunt called out.

"Damn it. How far out is our extract?"

"Too far."

"All right then, dig in. We hold here. Striker, you've got Mel. No one gets her."

"Understood."

———

The 416 in Kane's hands fired once more and a shooter using a building for cover disappeared with a cry of pain. The small group were now forted up in a building small enough to be held comfortably provided they could keep their ammunition supply intact.

Rucker finished bandaging Borden Hunt's arm wound and said, "That'll see you through, Bord."

"Thanks, kid."

"I've got movement on my corner," Striker called out. "Maybe they're going to try and rush us again."

All around the building lay corpses of the attackers. Kane figured at least ten of them. But there were more out there.

"Rucker, find out what's keeping our extract," Kane said looking at his watch. "They should have been here five minutes ago."

"On it, Reaper."

Kane turned and looked at the man tied in the corner. The guy resembled a normal Texas cowhand who'd come in off the range. Kane got to his feet and walked over to him. The right leg of his jeans was covered in blood from the bullet wound he'd received.

"Who are you people?" Kane asked him.

The man looked up at him. "Never mind who we are, traitor."

Kane raised his eyebrows. "I'm a traitor?"

"Yeah, you people are responsible for the death of the VP and the director of the CIA."

Hunt heard the exchange. "Pal, you've got it all wrong. We worked for him. Alex Joseph was our boss. You want to know who is responsible for what happened, look at the man in charge of the country."

"Bullshit."

"Joseph was killed because he was onto them."

"What about the VP?" the man snarled.

"I don't know, but there has to be a reason."

"Yeah, I'm looking at it."

"Damn it, you dumb son of a bitch, we weren't even in the same state when he was killed."

"You don't have to be."

Hunt was about to punch him in the mouth when

Kane said, "Forget it, Bord. He's only spouting what he's been told."

"It would make me feel better."

Kane's attention went back to the wounded man. "Who do you work for? You're not official, which means you're paramilitary. You're Texan which makes me think Jack Harding."

Jack Harding, AKA The Texas Tornado. Harding made his fortune working security after the early days of the second Iraq war. It had not taken long to earn enough money to start his own firm which only grew from there. Now he was one of the biggest defense contractors in the US.

"You work for that asshole?" Hunt asked.

"He is a true patriot," the wounded Texan hissed.

"Maybe at one stage he was. Not anymore."

"What would you know?"

"I'll tell you what I know. I was leading a team in East Africa five years back when I came across a small village his goons paid a visit to. There was nothing left. He'd been hired to do a job by the current government there, and he did it by massacring everyone.

"The other thing that people don't know," Kane added, "is that one Randall Coster is a major share-holder in the company."

"You're all full of horse shit," the wounded man growled.

"They wouldn't have found us on their own," Kane theorized. "Who helped you?"

"Fuck you."

Kane kicked him in the wounded leg. He was beyond being nice. The man cried out. "Try again," Kane snarled.

"What are you doing?" the Texan blurted out.

"Who helped you?"

"Shit, it was Forest. He's running the show, we're just extra muscle."

"Trent Forest?"

"That's right."

"Wow, the biggest mercenary of them all."

"Reaper, extract is inbound. Two mikes out," Rucker called to him.

The next voice he heard was Striker's. "Reaper, we've got incoming vehicles from the west. Armed Humvees."

"All right, back to work. Rucker, let the extract team know they've got a hot LZ."

"Roger that."

Kane checked his magazine and then hurried across to a window. There were four of them, all in a line. He could see the men manning the rooftop machineguns, taking particular note of the lead vehicle with the .50 caliber weapon sited on it.

"Target the fifty," Kane said.

As one, the group opened fire at the lead vehicle and Kane saw the bullet strikes as it was peppered. Then the operator on the heavy machinegun jerked and disappeared within the vehicle.

The other gunners in the three trailing Humvees opened fire and hammered the building with lead.

Kane ducked down as the rounds punched through the walls into the interior. He heard someone cry out in pain and turned. He saw Striker down, wounded for a second time. Only this one was worse than the previous one.

"Scimitar, Striker's down hard!"

"Rucker, check him," the former SEAL shouted.

Rucker broke away and ran to the fallen man. He checked Striker and took only seconds to arrive at his diagnosis. As he ran back to his post he yelled, "He's gone."

Kane cursed savagely. That was two gone. Ruggles and Striker. Add to the mix Anvil and Joseph, and someone was going to pay. He dropped out the almost empty magazine and did a tactical reload.

The 416 came up to his shoulder and he opened fire once more. The almost overwhelming incoming rounds were starting to suppress the shooters, forcing them to the floor of the building they were in. It was only a matter of time before more men were able to get inside and the battle would be done.

All of a sudden, one of the vehicles exploded as a helicopter zoomed overhead. Kane had no idea where it came from, but he was happy to see it.

"That's it, Reaper," Rucker called out. "That's our ride out of here."

The Black Hawk helicopter came back around and opened fire once more. However, it was soon joined by an MH6 little bird. This one had rocket pods on the side. The rockets darted out like long lances destroying whatever they touched. Then the mini guns opened fire and a hailstorm of bullets danced across the concrete apron.

"Great. We've got to go out the back. The Black Hawk is touching down out there now."

"What about Ruggles and Striker?" Hunt shouted over the din.

"We have to leave them. They'd understand."

"Fuck."

"Rucker, get Melanie."

"Copy, Reaper."

Moments later, while the little bird kept up its hurricane rate of fire, the surviving members who'd been on the ground since the operation to get Kane's sister from her prison hurriedly climbed onto the Black Hawk.

As soon as they were all aboard, the machine lifted its skirts and then turned to the right before flying for a notch in the surrounding hillsides where it disappeared.

CHAPTER 4

LA GUAIRA, VENEZUELA

CARA SLIPPED between two stacks of shipping containers and stopped at the opening. Brick was close behind her, and he leaned his back against the container opposite to where she stood. Both had out their Glock 17s.

"Bravo Four, copy?" Cara said into her comms.

"Read you loud and clear, Reaper Two."

"What are you looking at, Slick?" she asked.

"The ship you are looking for is berthed down to your left possibly one-hundred meters away," Swift replied. The Bravo element was still airborne, but Swift was working his magic with a laptop and a satellite link.

Cara eased her head around the corner of the container and looked along the dock. The ship was there alright. It was stern on, and she could just make out the name of it in the light which shone from the large poles situated on the dock itself.

Reaching into her coat Cara took out a small pair of binoculars. She lifted them to her eyes and observed what was happening. The ship had an inboard crane which was steadily unloading a container.

Cara moved the binoculars to see if there was a number on the side. "Slick, what were the numbers we're looking for?"

Swift ran through a container number. Cara listened and then said, "That's not it. Tell me the second one."

She waited, listening. Once he had run through the list, she gave an abrupt nod. "That's the first one."

"Well, there's one more there somewhere."

"And your intel says that the meeting is tomorrow night?" she asked.

"That's right."

Suddenly three bouncing sets of headlights came towards them along the dock. Cara took a breath and said, "Get a look at this, Brick."

The team's combat medic leaned out and using his own binoculars studied the approaching vehicles. "If I was a gambling man, I'd say the meeting has been moved up a day."

"Shit! Shit! Shit! This can't be happening. Bravo Four, copy?"

"Roger."

"Is Zero with you?"

"Wait, Two."

Cara stared at Brick. "We have to go operational, now. Reach out to Knocker and Axe. Have them get the van and everything we need ready and on the move. I want them here in ten."

"It's a twenty-minute drive, Cara."

"Not if Knocker drives. Tell him to haul ass."

"Yes, ma'am."

"Reaper Two, this is Zero," Ferrero said as he came on. "Go."

"Luis, it looks like the meeting is going down now. I'm mobilizing the team to move on the shipment."

"Copy, Reaper Two. Good luck. We'll monitor things from here."

"Roger that. Out."

Cara leaned back out and watched as the three vehicles rolled to a stop and those inside climbed out. Six looked to be bodyguards, the seventh was a man dressed in a suit whom they knew all too well. Brett Edison.

"Slick, can you zoom in with that satellite of yours and get some pictures here on the ground?"

"On it."

"Zero, it looks like we've got our chicken in the hen house."

"Roger."

From where she watched, Cara could see Edison talking to a man she'd never seen before. "Slick, I need an ID on the guy Edison is talking to."

"I'll try, ma'am."

"Reaper Two, Bravo. Go to a secure channel."

She glanced at Brick who looked confused. Cara changed to the backup channel and said, "Go, ma'am."

"Reaper Two, we've just received word that Kane has been evacced from Point Echo along with his sister and two others."

Cara felt a wave of relief wash over her. "Good news, ma'am."

"Yes, but I'm afraid there's more. They lost Ruggles and Striker. I don't know the details."

"Thank you, ma'am. I'll sit on the information until the time is right. What is Reaper's destination?"

"He's coming south. We can expect him in country within twenty-four hours."

"Yes, ma'am. It'll be good to have him back."

"Indeed. Now, the arms shipment. I want it taken in transit. Let Edison leave. The prize will be the shipment in Africa."

"Yes, ma'am."

"Good luck. Bravo out."

The net went quiet, and Cara changed back. "Zero, Reaper Two back on channel."

"Copy, Reaper Two."

"Reaper Two, copy?"

"Copy, Bravo Four."

"I have an ID for you on the tango. He is Lucero Perez. Our friend is the rebel leader in country."

"Copy. Zero, I need a confirmation order for Perez, over."

"Wait one." A few moments later Ferrero said, "Use discretion, Reaper Two. If he gets in the way, then you are cleared to take him down."

"Roger that. Slick, copy?"

"Yes, ma'am."

"I need you to put your thinking cap on and give me a best guess on the route they're going to take."

"Not asking much, Reaper Two."

"Like I said, best guess."

"Yes, ma'am."

Cara turned her attention back to the meeting. "Now we wait."

———

Perez closed the lid on the crate of rocket launchers. "Good. The money will be transferred in a few moments."

Edison smiled at the bearded man. "It has been a pleasure doing business with you, Lucero."

"What about the other thing we discussed?"

"They are still on the ship. They will lead your men in the operation, and after that, the rest is up to you."

"Thank Mister Harding for me."

There was a commotion behind them, and Edison looked over his shoulder. Coming down the gangway was a line of men, around twenty in total. All were armed and carried rucksacks. They were Jack Harding's men from his security agency. Their mission was to work alongside the rebels and help them in their planned coup. Once that was achieved and the rebels held power, Randall Coster would deploy assets into the country to tap the newly discovered oil field at a price already discussed with Perez.

Coster and his compatriots were the real power. They ran a shadow-like government, out of sight of prying eyes. Once the new elections were held they had bigger plans to implement. The Venezuelan project was just the beginning.

Next on their list was Sierra Leone; a large diamond deposit that the Chinese had their eye on and were negotiating with the current government for access. This was the reason the shadow government were supporting the rebel faction to stage a coup. Only this one required more arms and timing.

Then there was Taiwan. Considered to be the jewel in the crown. They'd been working on it for the past few years since the Chinese had begun developing Next Gen fighters. They had been supplying the People's Liberation Army Airforce with new microchips for them. What the Chinese didn't know was that once the chips were activated remotely, their Next Gen fighters would be falling from the sky. This would leave them with only their antiquated planes to use in any form of aggression. Without their fighter capability, they would be left vulnerable.

All this would come to a head when the United States announced that they were going to base multiple fighter wings on Taiwan itself. This was designed to bring on an open conflict. Richard Nelson just didn't know it yet.

Edison turned to the man leading the team. "Lester, a word."

The man walked over to Edison. "What is it?"

"Keep everyone on their toes. Something isn't right, and I don't know what it is."

"Yes, sir."

"Give them a hand loading the arms. The sooner they're off the dock, the better."

———

"That was interesting," Cara said.

"Private security contractors," Brick said. "Can see it a mile away."

"Yes, but whose, and what are they doing here?" She pressed her transmit button. "Bravo Four, I need some intel on the new arrivals."

"Already on it, ma'am. Your new friends are in the employ of Jack Harding, the Texas Tornado."

"Now why do you suppose they're down here?" Cara asked.

"Not sure, ma'am, but according to reports, Kane and the others had some issues with the same crowd at Point Echo before extraction."

"Roger. Reaper Three, where are you?"

"Two mikes out, and closing."

"Hold position."

"Ma'am?"

"I said hold position."

"Yes, ma'am."

Cara and Brick continued to watch the weapons being loaded. When the job was almost done two more trucks arrived. This was transport for the contractors.

Brick said, "Ma'am, we can't take the shipment with all those contractors there."

She nodded. "It certainly creates a problem."

———

"Four against thirty," Knocker said. "I'm thinking that they're terrible odds for the defending team."

"You have a plan, Knocker?" Cara asked. After a few minutes, Cara decided to trust Swift with the surveillance of the weapons shipment, and left to rendezvous with the others.

"I was thinking that we could run away."

"Good plan. What do we have?"

"The FNs, our sidearms, some grenades—"

"What about explosives?" Cara asked.

"Just what we have to blow the weapons," Knocker said.

"Forget it. I have another plan. IED. We blow it as the convoy passes."

"We don't know which way they're going to track," Axe reminded her.

"We use our own vehicle. Make it mobile."

They all looked at each other. Knocker nodded. "Fuck it. This little black duck wasn't meant to live forever."

Cara smiled. "Can you rig something?"

The Brit grinned. "Making things go boom is my specialty."

"Get to it." Cara walked away from the others and said, "Zero, copy?"

"Roger, Reaper Two. Send traffic."

"We've come up with a plan but will need some kind of extract."

"No can do, Two. You know the parameters."

"Copy. How is the shipment looking?"

"They won't be long now."

"Roger, out."

For the next ten minutes Knocker worked until he had the second of their two vehicles ready. "We're right to go. It should make a big bang."

"Right. Bravo Four, I need a route."

"Reaper Two, we'll send it to you."

Two heartbeats later, Cara had what she needed. A minute after that, the team was gathered around her as she worked the tablet with the map.

"The blue line is the most likely route out. However, by the looks of it, this point here is the best place for ambushing it." She touched the screen and made it bigger. "If we put the IED here then we should get maximum effect."

Knocker nodded. "I agree. Then we set up in these four places and we should be able to extract when we need to."

"Sounds like a plan."

"Let's get mobile."

CHAPTER 5

LA GUAIRA, VENEZUELA

WELCOME TO VENEZUELA, a tropical country with crazy politics and where shit will go wrong when you least want it to.

"Reaper Two, the convoy has turned. I say again, the convoy has turned."

"What do you mean, turned?"

"They chose a different route."

"Everybody into the vehicles now," Cara said into her comms.

"What are we going to do?" Knocker asked.

"We're going after that damn convoy."

"We are?"

"Yes, Knocker, we are. You're with me."

They broke cover from their various hiding positions, Cara running straight towards the IED vehicle. Knocker was close behind her. They all wore masks as well as body armor. "If you're doing what I think you are doing, I'm driving."

Cara looked at Knocker. "What is it you think I'm doing?"

"Just get on, ma'am."

The vehicles fired up and soon they were on the street, one following the other. "Where are they going?" Knocker asked Slick.

"Turn right at the end of the street, Reaper Four," came the reply.

Knocker turned the wheel, and the vehicle responded, taking the corner at a rate of knots. His foot went to the floor as it sped up in the darkness, no street-lamps to guide their way.

Swift's voice came back over the comms. "Up ahead there is a roundabout. You need to go through it and then take your next left."

The Brit barely slowed as he took the roundabout. Cara, in the passenger seat, hung on for dear life. "You do realize that this is a fucking IED on wheels, don't you?"

"Trying not to think of it at the moment, ma'am."

"That's great." She said, "Brick, drop back a bit, just in case this lunatic blows us all up."

"Don't you have faith in me?" Knocker asked.

"Oh, I have plenty of faith. I'm just not sure whether it's misplaced or not."

Knocker grunted. "Talk to me, special one."

"You've got a T junction ahead of you. Turn right."

Knocker slowed the vehicle this time. He turned right, and once more his foot went down hard on the gas pedal.

"How far away from them are we?" Cara asked.

"That depends, ma'am. What is it you're trying to do?"

"We're going to hit the convoy."

"Repeat please."

Knocker said, "Let me make it a bit clearer for you, sunshine. We're going to ram this vehicle into the convoy and then we're going to blow it up."

There was a drawn-out silence before a voice came back over the comms. "Reaper Four, are you feeling alright?"

Knocker glanced at Cara. "I don't think the boss likes our idea."

"It is the only way to intercept, ma'am," Cara said.

"It's a damned stupid idea if you ask me."

"Good thing we never asked you then, isn't it?" Knocker shot back at her.

"Turn left, turn left!" Swift's voice was urgent.

Without thinking, the Brit swung on the wheel. The rear of the vehicle slid out before the tires bit and it shot forward again. "Shit, Slick. What was that about?"

"Up ahead was a dead end. You would have run into a brick wall, literally."

"OK."

"You should intercept shortly. Be ready. At the next intersection, turn right, then go ahead for 500 meters."

Knocker made the turn. Beside him, Cara checked the magazine on the FN. She pulled her mask down and said, "Everybody get ready."

"Bravo Four, copy?"

"Roger that."

"Listen, Slick, I need to know that when we get to the end of this street, we are going to actually intercept the column."

"Should put you on a path to hit dead center, ma'am. If you keep your present speed."

"Thank you. I'll get back to you when we're finished. Out." She glanced across at Knocker. "It's up to you now. Just put it right in the middle of it."

The Brit pulled his mask down. "Get ready to bail, ma'am."

The vehicle bounced along the street, hitting the occasional pothole, doing the suspension no favors. The distance between them and the intersection ahead grew smaller and smaller.. Then with about 100 meters left to go, they each put their hands on the doors and opened them. Knocker placed his weapon across his lap just before he jumped.

80 meters. 60 meters. 40 meters. 30 meters.

"Out!" Knocker shouted as he leaped from the driver's seat. He hit the pavement hard as the vehicle kept on going. He rolled over three times before coming to a stop.

The mobile IED shot out into the intersection and smashed into one of the trucks as it went by. Knocker reached into his pocket, pulled out the remote detonator, and then hit the button.

The explosion was massive. An orange ball of flame shot skyward, high above the rooftops of the dwellings along the street. Windows were blown out from the concussive force of the blast. The next truck in line was also engulfed in the explosion.

It was all made worse by the ammunition and the rocket propelled grenade rounds, which were stored in crates in the back of both vehicles.

Knocker felt the air crushed from his lungs. They had been way too close. Stunned, he looked around, trying to find Cara. He saw her across the street, her unmoving form sprawled face down. Still unable to take his feet, he crawled across to her.

She was unconscious. Maybe it was from the blast or the fall from the truck. He couldn't tell. He gently tapped the side of her face and rolled her onto her back. "Come on, lass. Wake up. We don't have time for this."

She remained silent.

"Come on, Cara, wake up."

She moaned. Her head moved from side to side. Knocker said into his comms, "Brick, Axe, you still there?"

"Copy, Knocker."

"Come and pick us up. The boss is down."

"Is she alright?"

"She's just had the stuffing knocked out of her. She'll be fine. Just come and get us."

"Be right there."

The second vehicle roared up the street towards where they lay. Brick helped them both into the vehicle while Axe covered their movements. Once they were loaded, Axe fell back to the vehicle.

"Reaper Four, you have hostiles moving in your direction," Swift said. "Confirm five. I think they're doing a sweep."

"Shit, that's just great," said Axe throwing his hand in the air.

Suddenly the night erupted with gunfire and bullets snapped close to the big former recon marine. He whirled and returned fire, blowing through a magazine in no time. He then dropped out the spent one and slapped home a fresh one.

Axe brought the FN back up and opened fire again.

"Are you coming, big man?" Brick said over the comms.

"On my way." He turned and took two steps before he grunted, staggered, and then kept moving to the vehicle.

Axe climbed in and slammed the door.

"Are you alright?" asked Brick.

"Yeah, drive."

Brick slammed the stick into reverse and the vehicle shot backward in a hurry. Bullets hit it as it moved, sounding like they were driving through an afternoon storm full of large hail.

While Knocker checked on Cara in the front, Axe slumped to the left, resting his head against the door pillar. "Axe, are you going to shoot back?" Brick asked.

"Yeah, just give me a minute while I get my breath."

The former SEAL glanced at the Team Reaper operator. "Hey, buddy, are you alright?"

"I'm fine, just tired."

"Shit. Did you get clipped, Axe?"

"I—yeah, maybe a little bit."

"Motherfu—Knocker, check Axe."

"What?"

"Check Axe, he got clipped. He's blacking out. Most likely he's losing blood. I need you to check."

"Shit a brick." The Brit leaned over the seat. "Hey buddy, what's happening?"

"Let me sleep, stuff you. I'll be fine."

Knocker felt around. "Where'd you get hit?"

"What?" his head lolled to the side.

"Where'd the bullet get you, asshole?"

"In the back."

Knocker pushed him forward. He felt around and

his fingers located the moisture laden clothing. "Brick, he's losing a lot of blood. The bullet missed his plate."

"Find the hole and pack it with something. You have to stop the bleeding."

The Brit worked feverishly on the big man doing his utmost to save his life. "Axe, old cock, are you still with me?"

Axe mumbled something about being tired.

"Don't bullshit me, old son, you're tougher than that."

"Reaper Three, what's happening, over?" Ferrero asked.

"We've got a Reaper hit, boss. He's bleeding badly."

"What's his status, Reaper Three?"

"Fuck...priority one, Zero."

"I was afraid you were going to say that. Can Five do anything for him?"

"I don't frigging know," Knocker said curtly. "Just leave me to work here."

"Copy."

"Talk to me, Knocker," Brick said.

"He needs a medivac, Brick," Knocker said with finality. "He's hit hard."

"We'll get him back to base and I'll be able to assess him there. What about Cara?"

"She's still pretty much out to it. I'd say heavily concussed."

For the next few minutes Knocker worked to stem the flow of blood from the big Marine. Then, "No, no, no, no."

"What's wrong?"

"He's got no pulse."

"Shit," Brick hissed and pulled the vehicle over. He

started to do his thing and within moments he knew and stopped.

"What are you doing, Brick? Keep working, pal."

"He's gone, Knocker." Brick's voice was low, almost hoarse.

"The fuck he is, do something." The Brit's tone was demanding.

"He's gone, Knocker. There's nothing left to do."

"*Fuck!*"

Ferrero's voice came over the comms. "Reaper Three, sitrep."

Silence.

"Reaper Three, sitrep, over."

Silence.

"Zero, this is Reaper Five. We've got a man down hard, I say again, we've got a man down hard. Returning to base."

There was another moment of silence before Thurston came on the comms. "Define 'hard,' Reaper Five."

"He's priority four, ma'am. We lost Axe."

———

GEORGETOWN, GUYANA

"Confirm your last, Reaper Five."

"You heard me right, ma'am. We're returning to base."

Thurston turned to look at Ferrero. "You heard that, right?"

He nodded. "Affirmative. Shit."

The former general stared at the floor as a heavy

silence descended over the room. It wasn't the first time the team had lost someone, but it was the first time Thurston had lost one of the team. "Damn it, Axel."

"Mary, might I suggest we get them out as soon as possible?" Ferrero said as he looked around at the rest of Bravo.

She nodded stoically. "Yes, do it."

"Carlos, see to it."

"Right away," the Mexican said with a nod.

Ferrero turned to the others. "Listen up."

They all gathered round to face him—Brooke Reynolds, Pete Teller, Traynor, the former DEA undercover, Swift, and Rosanna Morales, the team doctor.

Ferrero continued, "I know this comes as a shock to you all, but we don't have time to grieve right now. The team is still in the field, and we need to get them home. If Carlos comes to you for help, give him whatever he needs. Understood?"

They all nodded.

"Right, get it done."

He turned back to Thurston. She said, "Someone should tell Reaper."

Ferrero sighed. "I'll do it."

———

LA GUAIRA, VENEZUELA

Cara stared at the body bag in the corner, her head pounding from the concussion. A tear slid down her cheek as she remembered her lost teammate. Even worse, he'd been lost on her watch. She took a pull at the beer she'd been drinking then placed it against her forehead, allowing the coolness to penetrate her skull.

"Damn it, Axe, why did you have to go and do this?" she said softly.

"Because he forgot to duck," a voice said from behind her.

Cara turned her head and saw Kane standing in the doorway. Her single tear turned into a flood as her eyes overflowed. All the pain she felt within became etched on her face. "Oh, John, I'm so sorry."

She came to her feet and went to him, swept up in his arms, pressing her face to his shoulder. "It's all my fault, John."

"Hey," he said softly. "Axe was a warrior. He knew what could happen every time he went in harm's way. But he still went. It's not your fault and he'd say as much to you if he could."

"It was on my watch."

"Could have happened on mine, Cara." He tilted her head up and kissed her on the lips. He tasted the saltiness of her tears. "Not your fault, OK?"

She nodded. "OK."

He kissed her forehead. Cara said, "I'm glad you're back safely."

There was movement behind them. "Thought I saw you sneak in," Knocker said. He held out a beer.

Kane reached for it and took a drink. "Thanks."

"Prick of a situation, Reaper."

"It's been better. What's the word?"

Cara stepped back. "They're getting us out of here as soon as they can."

"Roger that."

"Now, tell me what we're looking at," Kane said.

"We managed to hit the shipment and destroy it. That was how Axe was killed. We also saw about twenty of Jack Harding's operators get off the ship."

This piqued Kane's interest. "Any idea what they're doing here?"

Cara shrugged. "Training the rebels, maybe."

"It would make sense, I guess. Anything else?"

"Not really. What about you?"

"You know about our losses?" Kane asked.

Cara nodded. "They're coming after everybody hard."

"Led by Trent Forest and his mercenaries," Kane said. "Somehow Randall Coster is involved as well."

"What do we do?" Knocker asked.

"Stay the course. Complete the mission."

"That means we go to Africa," Knocker said.

"Where?"

"We don't know yet. I guess they'll tell us once we get out."

"I guess so."

────────

The SUV rolled to a stop and the headlights went out. Behind it were six more that followed suit. In the lead vehicle the driver said, "That's it, over there."

"Are you sure?" asked Forest as he stared at the abandoned trucking company yard.

"Yes, they are there. The windows are blacked out."

Forest reached for his radio handset. "Everyone out."

Doors opened and shooters disengaged from the vehicles. Forest followed their movements and eased the SUV's door shut. Bill Knowles came up to him and said, "How do you want to play this, Trent?"

"Cut a hole in the fence and take your team around the back. Keep Harding's men in reserve. I don't know them, and I don't want them shooting us by mistake."

"Copy."

"Let me know when you're in position."

Forest had called more shooters in for the assignment. There was too much money involved not to. He watched Knowles take five shooters with him towards the fence where they paused long enough to cut their way through.

Using hand signals, Forest gathered his team around. "We're going in. Crypto, you're on point. We ingress where Bill's team just went through. From there we circle around to the main entrance and breach there."

"Sure thing, boss," Crypto replied.

"Move out."

———

"Someone just breached the perimeter fence," Watson said hurriedly to Kane and Cara. "Motion sensors just went off."

"Time to go to work," Kane said coming to his feet.

Moments later the team were gathered, armed, and wearing their tactical gear. Watson was hunched over a computer screen. "You've got one group moving around the rear of the building and a second approaching the front. Twelve shooters altogether."

Kane stared at the grainy screen and saw what Watson had been watching. The shooters were moving professionally, well-trained. Then, when they reached the front entrance of the main warehouse, one of them looked up at a camera placed there. Kane shook his head. "Son of a bitch."

"What is it?" Cara asked.

"Trent Forest. This is going to hurt."

Cara checked her weapon. "Knocker and Brick, take the back; Reaper and I will take the front."

Knocker punched his chest and said, "Let's get some."

Kane looked at Watson. "Is there another way out?"

Watson said, "Use this place as your fallback area. I'll get you out."

Kane nodded. "Let's do it."

———

Knocker dropped out his magazine and replaced it with a fresh one. Gunfire rattled noisily throughout their section of the warehouse, bouncing off the walls. He and Brick were sheltered behind an old trailer with flat tires and a rusted frame.

Bullets ricocheted off the trailer from a shooter. Knocker returned fire and forced him back into cover. "Things are getting iffy around here," Knocker said.

"They're well trained," Brick replied.

"And we're at the bottom of our game. Shit." He fired again. "Reaper, copy?"

"Go ahead, Knocker."

"We need to get the fuck out of here before we wind up dead."

"No, we hold."

"Damn it, that's not the way. We get out and regroup."

"Who is in command here?" Kane growled.

"That isn't the issue," the Brit shot back at him. "The issue is us all getting killed because we're off the boil."

"Stand where you are."

"*Fuck!*"

Knocker stood up and emptied another magazine. "Hold onto your hat, Brick."

Brick stared at him and asked, "What the hell was that?"

"Zero, copy?" Knocker said into his comms.

"Roger."

"Is the boss there?"

"I'm here, Reaper Three," Thurston said.

"Either you pull rank on this thing or you're going to lose more people. Your choice."

"Knocker, what the hell are you doing?" Kane snarled over the open channel.

"What needs to be bloody done. You're not seeing things clearly at the moment. We need to fall back."

"Just do your—"

"Reaper One, get your people out of there," Thurston said, cutting across the on-air argument.

"Say again, Bravo."

"Get out. That's an order."

There was a pause before Kane said, "Roger that. Everyone fall back."

Brick gave Knocker an "I'd hate to be in your shoes" look. The Brit shrugged and mouthed, "Screw it."

They fell back to where Watson waited for them. He already had a trapdoor open for their exfil. When

Kane turned and saw Knocker, he said nothing but punched him in the mouth.

The Brit shook his head and glared at him. "That's one, cock. You won't get another."

"That's all I need. Once we're done with this mission, you're gone."

"Fine by me."

Before it could go any further, Cara stepped in between them and said to Kane, "Get down that frigging hole, now."

The man they called Reaper turned and started to descend. Cara turned to Knocker. "Last man, watch our six."

"Yes, ma'am."

"And be careful."

Brick appeared carrying the body of Axe over his shoulder. He was a big man, and strong, but even he was showing the strain. "Watson, give us a hand."

"Christ," whispered Cara. "I'd forgotten about him."

They wrestled the body-filled body bag down through the opening then disappeared. More gunfire erupted from out in the main building. Cara pressed her talk button. "Knocker, you're it."

"Don't wait for me, ma'am. I'll be along."

"Don't let me down, Raymond."

"Wouldn't dream of it."

Cara climbed down into the tunnel. It was illuminated by a string of bare light globes along the length of the tunnel. Brick and Watson had gone on ahead, leaving Kane waiting for her. "What the blazes was that?" she growled at him.

"It was disloyal," Kane snapped.

"He did the right damn thing because you weren't thinking straight, and *we*...we as a team don't have our heads in the game."

"Bullshit. The team is fine."

"The team lost a friend. We're not OK. I'm not OK. Now move."

———

Knocker knew he'd left it too late. The attackers were closing in on him and he was about to be pinned down. Oh, and run out of ammunition.

"Where are you, Reaper Three?" Cara asked.

"Not far away. Keep going. I'll be there shortly."

"You don't even know where there is, Knocker," she pointed out.

"I've still got my uplink."

"Roger. Good luck."

The FN ran dry just as a shooter exposed himself to press forward. Knocker let out a curse, threw the thing aside, and drew him sidearm. The Glock 17 hammered out three rounds and the shooter went down face first.

The Brit's actions brought forth an angry fusillade of fire which peppered his position. He hunkered down as debris fell upon him. Suddenly the shooting stopped, and a voice called out, "Why don't you give up before you die needlessly?"

"Ha, ha. Suck my dick," Knocker shouted back. "Wanker."

"Typical non-funny British humor."

"Stick your head out and I'll show you how funny I can be."

"Are you the sacrificial lamb?" the voice asked.

"The one thrown to the wolves so the others can get away?"

"That wasn't the plan. But I guess my timing kind of sucks."

"There is no way out for you. We don't want you. We want Kane."

"Bullshit, Forest."

"Well, you know my name."

"What happens if I give myself up?" Knocker asked.

"We will let you go after a few questions. That is all."

Knocker holstered his Glock. "All right. But if you shoot me after I come out, I'm going to be pissed."

"We will not do that."

"Fine, here I come. I'm unarmed."

"Just hold your arms out from your sides where we can see them," Forest ordered.

Knocker emerged from where he'd been hiding. His arms were out from his sides. His hands turned back, away from where Forest and his men stood. "Step forward slowly," the big mercenary said.

The Brit did as he was told, slowly, one step at a time. Then when he was close enough, Forest said, "That will do. Who are you?"

"Raymond Jensen. My friends call me Knocker."

"How British."

"What happens now?" Knocker asked.

"Now we kill you. Sorry, I lied."

"Thought as much," the Brit said.

Casually Knocker, turned his right hand around and then flicked his wrist forward. There was a dull thud as a fragmentation grenade landed on the concrete floor. A reply Axe was known to give when asked why he always carried a grenade, came into his head. "Never leave home without one."

Forest looked at the Brit and smiled coldly. "You are a ballsy prick."

Then everybody ran.

The explosion was loud inside the vast warehouse. Orange flame erupted towards the roof. The blast dislodging steel girders from above. Part of the building started to collapse, coming down on top of two of Forest's shooters. Their screams rang out.

But Knocker wasn't waiting. By that time Forest realized what was happening, and that Knocker wasn't there. The Brit was already going down the tunnel.

CHAPTER 6

GEORGETOWN, GUYANA

"THE TEAM IS clear and on their way to a secondary safe house," Ferrero said. "But we have another problem."

Thurston looked tired. She nodded and said, "It's certainly the day for it."

"Caracas is on fire. The Rebels are making their move and the whole place has become a battleground."

The former general looked confused. "Wait, I thought there was time. We destroyed the weapons."

"Looks like they're pushing ahead without them."

"Shit."

Ferrero had been carrying a folder. He took out a picture and placed it in front of Thurston. "There's this as well."

The photo showed a masked man leading what looked to be a squad of rebels. "What am I looking at, Luis?"

"The flash of skin around the wrist."

She nodded, looking closer. "Caucasian."

"Yes. It looks like, at a guess, Jack Harding's people are leading the rebellion."

"We have to let Hank know."

"Already done, Mary. He said to standby. News has already reached the British government and they're holding an emergency meeting."

"What does that have to do with us?" Thurston asked.

"Maybe Global have an idea that the embassy might need reinforcing," Ferrero theorized.

"God, I hope not. Our people have been through enough." Thurston sighed. "Did you pass on the intel we've managed to gather?"

"Yes."

"Good, let's see what they make of it. In the meantime, let's work on getting our people and Axe out."

Ferrero left Thurston and went to find Arenas. "How are things progressing with the extract?"

"I was just looking for you," the Mexican said. "Word has come through. Hank Jones wants them in Caracas. The embassy. Things are getting out of control. The Royal Navy has an assault ship and a frigate offshore but aren't willing to put troops into the mix just yet. They're going to dispatch a helicopter to pick up our people and put them on the embassy roof. Once they've done that, they'll take Axe's body back to the ship."

"I'll let Mary know." Ferrero paused. "How's everyone doing?"

"They're busy."

"Keep them that way."

"Will do."

LA GUAIRA, VENEZUELA

"We're being extracted by helicopter within the hour," Cara told Kane.

"Good. The sooner we're out of here the better."

"We're not going back," Cara said. "We're headed to Caracas. The embassy has requested assistance. Instead of Royal marines, they're sending us."

"You're kidding."

"No, not in the slightest. Axe will be taken back to the assault ship. He'll be repatriated from there."

Kane went silent at the mention of his friend and his mood darkened.

"Have you talked to Knocker?"

"Why? I've said all I've got to say. Once we're done, he's gone."

"You don't mean that, John."

He stared at her. She never called him John. "I do."

Cara's eyes flared. "You're a stubborn son of a bitch. And you're wrong."

He watched her storm off and went back to his thoughts.

The new safehouse was on the other side of La Guaira and boasted an area where the helicopter could pick them up. Watson would extract with them.

Cara went to seek out Knocker. She found him drinking a beer with Brick, and he came to his feet when she approached. "If you've come to chew my ass then get it over with. But just so you know, I'd do the same thing all over again if I thought it was the only option."

She nodded. "I know. I'm just checking to see how you're both doing."

"We're fine," Brick said. "What about Reaper?"

"He's...he's Reaper. Give him time."

"Time is something we don't have," Kane said appearing behind her.

Knocker turned to face him. "Reaper, I—"

"Don't talk to me," Kane growled. "I expect more from my people. Just get all your kit ready, we're out of here soon."

"Are you sure that's a good idea?" Knocker asked.

Kane glared at him. "If you've got something to say, say it."

The Brit nodded. "All right. You're not fit to command the team at this point. Not after what you've been through."

Kane lunged towards him, swinging a punch at Knocker's face. He blocked it and retaliated with one of his own, connecting with a blow to Kane's jaw but keeping a little in reserve.

"Whoa!" Brick exclaimed and stepped in between them, forcing them apart. "That's enough."

Knocker ignored him. "Come on, cock, have another fucking go. I'll put you into the middle of fucking next week."

"Get out of the way, Brick. It's time someone knocked some loyalty into him."

"*Enough!*" Cara's shout echoed throughout the room. "Knock it the fuck off."

They all stared at her.

"Yes, we're all hurting. Axe was our friend, but it wasn't anyone's fault what happened." She looked at Kane. "I know he was your friend, and you weren't here, but we all know what can happen every time we go out. Now, both of you, get your heads in the game before someone else gets killed."

Kane's jaw set stubbornly firm. "But—"

"He was damn right, Reaper. If he hadn't done it, I would have. You've been through a lot."

Silence once more.

Cara said, "Knocker, Brick, check your equipment. We're going into combat with stuff all, but I asked if they could resupply us from the ship. Get it done."

They nodded. "Ma'am."

She turned to Kane after the others were gone. "Now, give me a hug and get yourself sorted."

He wrapped his arms around her. "You're right. But I demand loyalty. Without it, we have nothing."

———

HEREFORD, ENGLAND

Hunt and Rucker stood in Hank Jones's office waiting for him to appear. "Pretty flash, Bord," Rucker said.

"Isn't it? Money does buy a lot of things."

The door behind them opened and Jones entered. "Find a seat, gentlemen, we have work to discuss."

They each took a chair and leaned towards the general's desk. Hunt said, "Good to see you, sir. Thanks for pulling us out."

Jones nodded. "Just a shame I couldn't get you all."

Hunt's expression was grim. "What is it you want us to do, General?"

"Well, first things first. Do you want to work for Global?"

The two men looked at each other. Rucker nodded and said to Hunt, "I'm with you whatever you decide, Bord."

"All right, we're in."

"Good. I want you to go to Taiwan."

Hunt frowned. "What's in Taiwan, sir?"

"Russell Frost."

"Who?"

"Russell Frost. Have you heard of Randall Coster?"

"Texas senator. As rich as they come."

"That's him. He's up to something and we need to find out why."

"How so, sir?" Rucker asked.

"Not sure. He's just been named as running for vice president in the next election. One out of left field. But he's on Nelson's ticket. Right after the last VP was assassinated. Coincidence, maybe, but when you add in Jack Harding's security forces showing up in Venezuela, it is suspect."

"I don't understand," Hunt said, a confused look on his face.

"Coster is a major shareholder in the company. They showed up along with a shipment of arms supplied to rebels by Brett Edison. If I had to guess, the weapons could well be out-of-date US stock. Team Reaper destroyed them, but the rebels have stormed into Caracas anyway with Harding's men leading them. Which means that Coster has his finger in it somehow. I want to know what he's up to. Frost will know."

"You want us to pick him up and question him?" Hunt asked.

"Yes."

"How aggressive do you want us to be?"

"Use your discretion, Bord," Jones replied. "Something is not right. Find out."

"Yes, sir, if he's tied up with Nelson and Edison, then we'll be happy to get to know him. Anything for the admiral."

———

WASHINGTON, DC

"It has started, Nelson," Coster said to the president. "The streets of Caracas are the most dangerous place on earth tonight if you are a supporter of the government."

"You seem to be enjoying this, Randall."

"I always enjoy it when I'm making money for my country."

Nelson picked up a remote and turned on the large flat screen television fixed to the wall. "Really? You call this making money? Our embassy which we just reopened in Caracas is under siege. So is the British."

"They will be fine. Our embassy will be evacuated before anything can happen. So will the Brits. They won't stay once we pull out."

"I hate to tell you this, but the Brits are going nowhere. I was just talking to their prime minister. He's talking of reinforcing their position."

"That's their bad luck."

"What I can't understand, Randall, is how this went ahead. The weapons were destroyed."

Coster nodded. "We had a contingency plan."

"What contingency plan?" Nelson asked cautiously.

"Two forces of private contractors were put ashore to lead the assault. One was to take control of the port of La Guaira. The other would help the rebels take the capital. So, even without the weapons, the rebels had the assistance they needed."

"Jesus Christ. You need to stop this."

Coster shook his head. "This doesn't stop until the completion of the operation in Taiwan."

Nelson froze. He stared wide-eyed at the man before him. "Taiwan?"

"That's right. The ultimate goal. The first two operations are to get under the skin of the Chinese. Taiwan is meant to push them over the edge."

"You mean to start a war with the Chinese?" Nelson asked, aghast.

"No, you will, and when you do, we will be able to eventually secure the South China Sea, and the Chinese economy will be in tatters and will have to rely on the US for help. All we need you to do is go to Taiwan and announce the arrival of two fighter wings which you will be deploying."

"You're crazy. Do you have any idea how many lives that will cost? American lives?"

"Not as many as if we didn't have other contingencies in place," Coster shot back at him.

"You keep talking of contingencies. What contingencies?"

"You don't need to know. Just do as you're told, and it will be fine."

"Until then?"

"Until then, we concentrate on our current operations and step up the rhetoric against China. The public must be onside when the time comes to go to war."

"It will take more than rhetoric to do that," Nelson pointed out.

"That's right. It will."

The screen on the television changed as though on cue, the headline banner at the bottom of the screen told the story.

"We have breaking news just coming in from unverified sources that a Boeing E-3 Sentry AWACS aircraft has been shot down by a Chinese fighter over the South China Sea while in international airspace. While..."

The phone on Nelson's desk started ringing as the president stared at the man before him. "What did you do?"

"What needed to be done. Now, control the situation until you are told not to."

———

HEREFORD, ENGLAND

Hank Jones studied the screen on the wall and started to wonder how much further the world was going to go down the shitter. Venezuela and now the South China Sea. Protesters were already gathering outside the Chinese consulate in Washington, and it was taking a sizable force of police to keep them back

Senators and congressmen and women were already calling for Nelson to move two more carrier fleets into the South China Sea as well as assault ships loaded with marines. The world was on the brink of war and only one man stood between it and peace.

The phone on Jones's desk rang. He picked it up. "Hank Jones."

"Hank, it's Richard Nelson."

Holy crap.

"Hank, are you there? I don't have much time."

"I'm here." There were no formalities. "What do you want?"

"To stop a war."

"Then you'd best get to it."

"Not without your help."

Jones snorted derisively. "Fuck off."

"I know, I deserve that but if you will give me a couple of minutes to explain, then I would be grateful."

"You'd best get busy then."

"Have you ever heard of Randall Coster?" there was a pause. "Of course, you have. He's leading a shadow government which is currently engaged in bringing China to war."

"Looks like he's already started."

"More than you know."

"And you are involved in this?" Jones asked.

"Up to a point, yes. I'm not involved with sending possibly thousands of young American men and women to their deaths."

"Go on."

"Venezuela and Sierra Leone are the tip of the iceberg. Small operations to get under the skin of the Chinese. The goal is Taiwan. Their theory is to bring China to war and destroy their economy so they will have to rely on the US."

"Then do something about it."

"I—I can't. It's complicated. Why do you think I'm

calling you? You are the only one I trust to be able to stop this."

"Trust?"

"Who can you trust if not your enemy?"

"What is their plan for Taiwan?" Jones asked.

"War. Coster keeps talking about contingency plans. However, he won't tell me what they are. If everything goes to plan, he will be the next VP. I fear that once that happens then the country is doomed."

"You lay down with dogs..." Jones muttered.

"Judge me all you want; it doesn't change things."

"Tell me this, who killed Alex?"

"That was them, the same with the VP. It is all them."

"All right, I'll look into it."

"Be careful, Hank. These people are like none you've ever dealt with before. They're cold, calculating. The AWACS, that was them as well."

Jones thought for a moment. The man was desperate. "Nelson, this is what you're going to do for me. If we manage to do this, you resign and confess to everything."

"Hank, I—"

"Not negotiable, Nelson. On top of that, you issue pardons for everyone of Team Reaper and their support crew."

"All right."

"How can I get in touch with you?"

"This number."

"Fine. But if this is a trap, then I will send them after you, Nelson. And you know what they can do."

The call disconnected and Jones leaned back in his seat. "Here we go again, saving the fucking world."

CHAPTER 7

CARACAS, VENEZUELA

THE HELICOPTER TOUCHED down briefly onto the roof of the embassy before lifting off again. It was sufficient time to disgorge its passengers, after which it headed back to the ship, swallowed by the darkness.

When the team had originally boarded, they found fresh armaments, ammunition, and all the equipment they would need, including night vision capabilities.

Head of security, Jack Olsen, met them. Olsen was a former Commando in another life. The big man still had dark hair, was wearing his own body armor and gear while carrying an L85A3 Assault Carbine.

The team on the other hand had been outfitted with M6A2s. All except Cara, who was carrying a HK 417 designated marksman rifle.

"Good to see you people," Olsen said seriously. "I would have liked to have seen more of you."

"We're it," said Kane "What's the situation?"

"Take a look for yourself." The man indicated with a wide sweep of his arms.

They walked across the rooftop to a position overlooking the front gates. A large crowd was gathered outside shouting and waving sticks and iron bars. Further along the street a vehicle burned. Inside the reinforced iron gates stood three armed sentries. Kane said, "That gate won't hold if they ram it."

"Not a chance."

"Why didn't they evacuate?" Knocker asked.

"God knows," Olsen replied disdainfully.

"How many people do you have?"

"Ten men, three ladies, all combat trained."

"I don't get it," Brick said. "Why are they here?"

"They see us and the Yanks as collaborating with the current government. Therefore, that makes us the enemy. The Americans already evacuated. But not us, no way. We're British and it would be bad form."

"Fucking wankers," Knocker growled.

"Reaper, I have three Caucasian males walking around down there," Cara said as she swept the crowd with her scope. She passed the 417 over to Kane. "Two o'clock, one, and eleven."

"Got them. There is another back in a doorway across the street."

Kane returned the weapon to Cara. "Check the surrounding rooftops and—"

WHAP!

"Shit!"

They all dropped below the parapet, seeking shelter just in case another bullet reached out of the night. "I'm guessing there's a sniper out there somewhere," Cara said.

"Find him."

She went to work, and it was only a minute or so before she said, "Got him. Along the street, top of the building with the sign on it. Hiding in the crenellations."

"Can you get him?"

"I think so."

She firmly tucked the butt of the 417 in as she went through her routine. Then moments later the rifle whiplashed, and she said, "Threat neutralized."

They came back to their feet. Kane looked at Olsen. "Where do you want us?"

"I could use an extra one on the gate."

"Knocker, you're it."

"Copy."

"I'll stay up here, Reaper," Cara said. "Keep an eye on things."

He nodded.

Brick said, "I'll hang out here too."

"All right."

Olsen said, "You want to look around? We'll go over some things."

"Let's do it."

———

LA GUAIRA, VENEZUELA

The secure sat phone rang and Forest answered it. "Yeah?"

"I have a new mission for you in Caracas."

"I haven't finished this one."

"It can wait."

"What is it?"

"An extraction."

"From where?" Forest asked.

"The British embassy."

"I'll need transport."

"Being organized as we speak. You need to hurry."

"Why?"

"You'll see when you get there."

"Where will I find the target?"

The voice said, "In the basement. It is important that the package be brought out alive."

"Fine."

"I will send you everything you need."

———

CARACAS, VENEZUELA

The crowd had swelled, and it was starting to make the occupants within the embassy nervous. Spot fires were visible across the city and gunfire was becoming more frequent. Armored vehicles were reported to be in Plaza Francia, others at strategic points in the city. Roadblocks had been set up on Bolivar Avenue as well as Libertador Avenue.

The only problem was that men and equipment were defecting from the Venezuelan armed forces to the rebels.

News footage was starting to show bodies in the streets and civilians being taken off by armed men in plain vehicles.

Caracas was a city on the brink.

Kane and Olsen tried their best to strengthen the

defenses. They moved an armored vehicle across the gates, blacked out the windows, posted more shooters on the rooftop as well as other strategic places around the perimeter.

"Who do you have in the basement?" Kane asked.

"What do you mean?"

"I almost bought the story that because of the British relationship with the government was the reason why the crowd was concentrated here, but these people are openly hostile, bordering on the brink of being fanatical. Plus the fact it's growing all the time. In my experience, there is usually only one reason for that."

Olsen hesitated. "It's just as I said."

"Bullshit."

"It has to be, they can't know."

"Can't know what? Who is in the basement?"

"President Francisco Lopez and his family."

Kane glared at him and said into his comms, "Everyone on the roof now."

"The question is, what do we do?" Kane said.

"Whatever we can to protect them," Knocker said.

"That's right," agreed Cara.

"Brick?"

"I'd like to know how they found out."

"It doesn't really matter because it's only a matter of time before they get brave enough to come in here. What we need to do is get them out."

"In case you haven't noticed there's an angry mob out there," Knocker said.

"The only way is to get a helicopter."

"Good luck convincing Ambassador Welsh and the president that."

Kane said, "If we can't then a lot of people are going to die. Including us."

Knocker said, "If in doubt, fight like hell."

"Take me to the ambassador," Kane said. "Knocker, you're with me. Brick, front gate."

As they left the rooftop the Brit asked, "Does this mean I'm forgiven?"

"Not by a long shot. I just need your persuasive skills."

Olsen took them downstairs where staff were destroying documents, hurrying around busily like ants. "For people who aren't going anywhere, they sure look like they are," Knocker said.

They were shown into an office which was just as busy. The ambassador looked up and said, "What is it?"

Kane said, "I know about the president in the basement."

Welsh looked at Olsen and then back at Kane. "I don't know what you're talking about."

"We can play this game, but you don't have time. The people outside the gate know he's here, too."

"Impossible."

"To you it might be, but if we don't get him out of here then he and his family will all be killed."

"No one is going anywhere."

Knocker stepped forward. "Listen, you dumb prick. If we don't get him out of here that mob will kill him. Not only that, they'll rape his wife and his daughter. His son is his blood, so they'll kill him, too. Then they'll start on your staff. Do you want the responsibility for all that on your shoulders?"

"You don't understand. I've tried to get him to go. But he won't. All we can do is destroy sensitive documents and hope for the best."

"What about your staff?"

The ambassador shrugged.

"Love a fucking duck."

"Take us down to the basement," Kane said.

"I'll do no such thing."

"Damn it."

"Leave if you want to, but we're staying."

Kane turned to Olsen. "We're going to need more weapons."

"I've got them. What we need are bodies to use them."

"Leave that to me," said Knocker.

The former SAS man walked out of the ambassador's office and into the main area where the staff were busy. He climbed onto a desk and let out a piercing whistle stopping them where they stood. "All right, everyone's eyes on me."

They looked at him.

"Raise your hands if you've served in the military before."

Three hands went up.

"What about fired a gun, or had any type of training? Police maybe."

Four more hands.

"What are you doing?" the ambassador demanded.

"Anybody here from MI6?"

No one moved.

"Come on, don't be shy. I've worked out of places like this before." Knocker pointed at a woman in a pants suit. "You for certain."

She nodded. "All right, you got me."

"Who else?"

Another hand. A man.

"Great. You all just volunteered to serve your country. See Olsen and he'll set you up with weapons and ammunition."

"You can't do this," the ambassador protested.

Knocker grinned. "Just did, cock. You brought this on yourself when you wouldn't leave.

Olsen took Kane to the basement anyway. Outside the locked door of the safe room stood two men; inside there was another pair. Kane said to Olsen, "You might as well put these two to use on the perimeter. If the crowd gets in here, they'll be absolutely no use anyway."

The two men looked at Olsen who nodded. "Get going."

Lopez stepped forward. Kane had never seen the Venezuelan president before, and he was younger than expected. Maybe forty if he was lucky, handsome, with dark hair and eyes. "Who are you?"

"Hired help."

Lopez gave him a questioning stare. As he tried to decide what Kane was about, his wife, Carmen joined him. Kane caught his breath. The woman was exquisite. Almost perfect features, long dark hair, and a model's physique. And he wanted to keep her here in harm's way.

"I'm Carmen," she said. "Francisco's wife."

Kane nodded. "John Kane."

"What can we do for you, Mister Kane?"

"You can let me get you out of here," he replied. "Before the crowd gets in and kills you all."

Alarm came to her face, but she quickly composed herself. She grasped her husband's arm. "We will do what my husband decides."

Kane looked at the president. "Well?"

"We are staying. I will not run away from these terrorists."

"Yet here you are hiding in a basement," Kane said with sarcasm. "Go figure."

"You have my answer."

"Then you just condemned a lot of people to die, Lopez. Including your family. I hope you can live with that."

Kane didn't give him a chance to answer. He just turned and left.

Carmen Lopez followed him outside of the panic room. "Mister Kane, wait please."

Olsen gave him a look and said, "I'll see you upstairs."

Kane nodded. He stared at Carmen and asked, "What is it, ma'am?"

"Please don't judge my husband. He is a proud man. It kills him that he is hiding down here in the basement."

"Where is his security detail?"

"We left them behind. We didn't know who we could trust."

"Figures, I guess."

"Is what you said true? About them getting in?" she asked.

"Yes. We can only hold them for so long."

"I will try to persuade my husband to leave, but if I can't then I will stay with him."

"OK, it's your funeral, ma'am."

The comment darkened her face for only a moment before she composed herself once more. "One more thing, could you get me a sidearm?" He was about to say no when she added, "I served in the military before I met my husband. I am quite proficient in weapons handling."

Kane took his own out and handed it to her.

"I cannot take—" her protest was cut short.

"I'll get another," he said, handing her the spare magazines he had. "Good luck, ma'am."

———

Thirty minutes later the crowd was at fever pitch. It was into this chaos that Forest and his people arrived. The mercenary sought out the Harding contractor in charge, finding him in a doorway along the street, keeping a close watch over everything.

"They look like they're ready to go," Forest said.

"Any time, now," the man replied. "All they need is a little push."

Forest nodded his agreement. "I'll let you know when."

The man shrugged. "Just say the word. I've been directed to give you any help you need."

"How many people do you have in the crowd?"

"Five."

"Rebels?"

"Fifteen, maybe."

"All armed?"

"They will be when the weapons are passed out. Safer not to give them any until the last minute."

Forest understood the man's reasoning. "You'd better hand them out. We move in ten."

———

Knocker had swapped places with Brick, allowing the former SEAL to take up his position back on the rooftop where he could watch over Cara.

But it was Cara who came over his comms to issue the warning. "Reaper Three, I've got an uptick of armed tangos outside the wire. Standby."

"Roger that." He turned to the security men with him. "Heads up, gentlemen, the natives are about to try something. Anyone comes through those gates treat them as armed and dangerous."

"What if they're not?" asked a young man.

"I guarantee you, the first ones through those gates will be armed, mate."

Then something strange happened. The crowd parted as though forced apart. After which came a trail of smoke followed by a violent explosion as the gates were smashed open by an RPG.

Things had just escalated exponentially.

Knocker was knocked flat on the asphalt drive, the air whooshing from his lungs. With no time to waste, he forced himself to his feet, the M6 he had, sweeping around.

One of the security guards was dragging himself up off the ground, another, was rolling around, stunned from the blast. The third, the young man Knocker had just been talking to, was down hard, a piece of steel shrapnel buried in the back of his head.

"Shit!"

"Reaper Two, we need some cover, over."

"Got you, Reaper Three."

The crowd started to surge forward, and Knocker saw the armed men at the front. He brought the M6 to bear and stroked the trigger. He felt the familiar recoil as the carbine whiplashed. The first shooter went down, a bullet in his head.

From above, Cara fired and a 7.62mm round punched the ticket of another.

Knocker leaned down and grabbed the dead young man by the collar. He started dragging him away from the ruined gate while from the rooftop, more shooting could be heard.

The former SAS man looked over at the other security guards. The closest one looked at him and Knocker shouted, "Get here. Take him."

The guard grabbed the dead young man and kept going. Meanwhile, Knocker turned toward the gate and opened fire once more, downing another shooter.

"We can't hold them, Reaper Two. We're falling back."

"Roger, we'll cover you from here. Take up a secondary position. Don't let them inside."

"I can't promise that, but will do my best, ma'am."

———

Kane heard the explosion and then the exchange between Knocker and Cara. He said into his comms, "Knocker, you need to keep them out."

"Not sure that's possible, Reaper."

"Do what you can."

"Roger."

Kane looked at Olsen. "To the roof."

When they reached the top, he found the operators there deeply engaged. Cara was picking targets, but the wave of civilians was washing ashore through the gates like a tsunami.

"Reaper, we can't stop them. The shooters are mixed in and we can't hit most of them."

Kane's eyes darted back and forth. "Olsen, check in with the others."

He heard the head of security say, "All teams check in."

While they called in, Kane walked to the end of the rooftop to look at the street running along the other side. He frowned. Then suddenly he realized what he was looking at. A large hole in the fence. Scattered around it were the bodies of a small security detail.

"Kane, I can't raise team three," Olsen called out.

"They're down," Kane replied. "Knocker, we've got a breach to the east. I say again, breach to the east. We've got hostiles inside the wire."

———

Knocker heard the transmission and scowled. "You two stay here. I've got to check something out."

"Where are you going?" the bigger of the two guards asked, a hint of panic in his voice.

The former SAS man's eyes narrowed. "Just hold this position."

He whirled around and went inside. The foyer was

empty, the metal detector cubicles unmanned, desks empty. Instead of taking the stairs to the next floor, Knocker went to the left towards the east corridor. All along it were doorways, wood paneling, pictures. Every now and then a potted plant.

Knocker broke into a jog, turned a corner, before turning another. The hallway opened out into a large open plan office where staff were destroying documents like those their comrades were doing on the second floor.

He stopped near a gray-haired man. "Is there a way to the basement from here?"

"Through that door, along the hall, and turn right."

"Thanks."

Knocker burst through the doorway, all sense of safety for himself gone. He jogged along the hallway and turned right.

Gunfire rattled in the enclosed space and Knocker was forced to throw himself back or be ripped apart by a fusillade of bullets.

"Shit a brick."

He pressed himself against the wall and said into his comms, "I've got tangos in the basement, Reaper."

"Push through, Reaper Three. We're on our way."

"Roger."

Knocker changed hands with the M6 and leaned around the corner, firing a long burst. More gunfire rang out and bullets punched into the walls. The Brit returned it and then paused before firing again, just as the shooter appeared to fire his own weapon. The bullets from the M6 caught him flush, knocking him from his feet.

Keeping the weapon raised, Knocker moved

forward. No one appeared. The shooter had been posted as a sentry. Knocker opened the door at the end of the short hallway to reveal a g set of stairs to the lower level.

The Brit slowly went down them, step by step, his M6 ready, just in case. By the time he reached the bottom, he could hear the voices. An American. "Open the fucking door or I'll kill him."

A garbled response, and then the crack of a handgun.

Knocker ground his teeth together and exposed himself. The M6 rattled and shooters fell. He pressed forward, picking targets before they could respond to his presence. The last one to fall fired a single shot from a handgun.

Entering the small anteroom, the Brit made sure that all threats were down. One of the guards were down as well, the other still on his knees, unarmed, and trying to gather himself. "Are you good?" Knocker asked him.

The man hesitated.

"Are you good?"

"Y—yes."

"Get that door open."

"Why?"

"Because I said so."

Knocker started to check the fallen. He patted them down and then checked out their communications. He put an earwig in his ear and heard, "Damn it, Bill, talk to me."

"Bill's a bit fucked about now, but if you want, come check it out for yourself."

"Who is this?"

"My name is Raymond. Who are you?" The comms went dead. Knocker shrugged, "OK. Good talk."

Kane and Olsen appeared. The team Reaper commander looked at the dead operators. "Looks like you're good."

"We talked it over. Thing is, we need to get the HVT out of here."

"I agree, that's why there is a helicopter coming in from the *Heathrow*," Kane said. The *Heathrow* was the assault ship waiting off the coast. "Get them to the rooftop. That'll be our Alamo."

"Hate to point this out, mate, but everyone died at the Alamo. Including John Wayne."

"I'm no Duke, and I don't plan to. Get them moving."

CHAPTER 8

CARACAS, VENEZUELA

FOREST SEETHED WITH ANGER. He'd just lost a team of his most experienced operators led by Bill Knowles to no one special. Or that was what he was led to believe. Harding's men were still leading the rebels and the crowd had pushed into the embassy compound but were being held back by some well-placed defensive positions.

"Crypto, do you hear me?"

"Loud and clear, boss," the mercenary replied.

"Lead your team inside. Find that damn package."

"We're pinned down by the shooters on the roof," Crypto said. "Whoever they are, weekend warriors they're not."

"Find a way, damn it."

"We might be able to if you can keep their heads down."

"Give me a minute."

Where he was positioned on the rooftop opposite,

Forest was able to watch what was happening. Now he needed to do something.

He reached across and grabbed his Knight's Armament Company M110A3 Sniper system and brought it into his shoulder. He rested his cheek on the stock and then found a target through the AN/PVS-30 scope. At this range, with that vision, he couldn't miss.

Forest stroked the trigger and the first shooter dropped, causing the rest to seek cover. He said, "Crypto, move."

At the gates, Crypto and his five-man team pressed forward. Ahead of them in the doorway were the two guards that Knocker had left there. Crypto brought up his H&K 416 and fired, killing the first of them. Beside him, a teammate took out the second. "Trent, we're clear. Moving in."

Now that the way was clear, Forest moved. One of the first rules a sniper learns, don't stay in the same place too long.

Then he heard the helicopter.

The Chinook came out of the darkness and circled wide of the target building. Inside, Knocker could hear the *thump-thump* of the twin rotors as they fought to keep the aircraft up.

"Keep moving," he barked at the presidential family as they worked their way up the stairs.

As Lopez went past, he said, "This is ridiculous. I—"

"Shut up and keep moving, mate, or I'll leave your

ass here and take that beautiful wife of yours anyway. She's got more bollocks than you have."

The man glared at him, but Knocker didn't care; he was here to keep them alive, not make friends. And besides, the guy's wife was hot. He winked at her, and she smiled back at him, her teeth straight and white against her deep pink lipstick.

With Knocker taking point, the embassy security guard from the basement brought up the rear.

Gunfire erupted on the main floor. Knocker stopped them and peered around the corner of the stair-well landing.

He saw the shooters coming towards him. A team of five, maybe six, he couldn't tell. Immediately he knew what they were there for. He ducked back. "Shit."

Knocker took a deep breath and leaned back around, opening fire. A shooter fell. Dead? Maybe. It was hard to tell while he was hiding around the corner with bullets hammering into the wall.

He looked at the others using the walls for shelter. The two children, a boy and girl, looked terrified. Knocker smiled at them as he made a tactical change of the magazine in the M6. "How you doing, kids?"

They whimpered.

"Everything will be fine. Old Knocker is a whizz at helping people out. Why, I once helped the queen of England feed her Corgis. Now put your fingers in your ears, all right."

They followed his instructions. He looked at the others and said, "I'm going to lay down some fire and make them pull their heads in. You will take the kids and run across the hallway. Mucker, you first."

The guard nodded.

"Let's do it."

Knocker leaned out and opened fire once more. It was more for suppression than anything else. As soon as the former SAS man let loose, the guard ran across the narrow opening. Then he joined Knocker with more suppressing fire.

Knocker turned around. "Love, you go first with one of the kids. OK?"

There was an expression of steely determination on her face. She wrapped an arm around her daughter and raised the handgun that Kane had given her. Then without hesitation she guided the girl across whilst firing rounds from the weapon.

I'm in love, Knocker thought to himself.

The two shooters ducked back as another hailstorm of bullets buzzed along the hallway. Knocker looked at the Venezuelan President and then at his son. "Shit. Hey, cock, you go. I'll bring the kid."

"What?"

"Just go. Come here, kid."

"No."

"Come on, you'll be better off with me. I've got all the good bulletproof kit."

"No."

"Damn it."

The president pushed his son. "Andres, go. It will be fine."

However, when the kid moved, he ran towards his mother, not the Brit. "Good grief."

Knocker dived for the kid as he started across the open hallway. As he brought him to the floor, he turned his back, exposing it to the incoming gunfire. Two rounds hammered into the armor plates, knocking the air from his lungs.

"Bloody hell!" Knocker gasped and whimpered painfully.

The guard reacted straight away. He leaned out to grab Knocker when a burst of fire caught him, killing him instantly.

Next the president's wife, Carmen, moved. She grabbed Knocker by the collar and pulled with super-human strength. He slid across the floor, taking the kid with him.

Once in cover, he released the boy who dived into his mother's arms. The former SAS man came to his feet, gritting his teeth against the intense throbbing in his back. He looked at the woman and nodded. "Thanks."

Knocker checked the guard but found him unre-sponsive. He readied his weapon and said, "Get up the stairs to the rooftop. I'll hold them off."

The president looked as though he would argue but his wife glared at him. "Shut up and move."

They disappeared up the stairs while Knocker opened fire, driving the assaulters into cover. His maga-zine ran dry, but he hurriedly reloaded and gave them another burst.

Suddenly a dull thud sounded, and the Brit looked down to see a fragmentation grenade dancing at his feet.

"Oh, crap!"

The explosion rocked the building, not to mention the Brit. He felt the blast wash over him, pushing the air from his lungs. His ears rang and the room spun, turning things upside down.

Knocker started checking himself for wounds.

Finding nothing, he rolled over and tried to get to his feet. "No, not going to happen."

He rolled onto his back and drew his handgun. A shooter appeared around the corner through the lingering smoke and the Brit fired three shots.

The shooter reeled back, bullets hitting him in the chest and throat, blood spraying up the wall beside him.

Knocker dragged himself to his feet and started stumbling up the stairs towards the rooftop. Another shooter appeared below him and began firing.

Bullets kicked off the stairs and hammered into the walls. Over his comms, Knocker could hear calls coming in from Cara and Brick.

The whole of the embassy was now breached and the downstairs was starting to flood with hostiles. All those who could were now on the rooftop waiting for the helicopter to pick them up.

Knocker shot back as he climbed. The attackers were forced to take cover or meet the same demise as their comrade.

"Reaper Three, where are you? The helo is on final approach."

"I'm coming. Just have a few problems with the locals. Is the president there?"

"Roger that."

Suddenly the airwaves lit up.

"...president is down..."

"...package is hit..."

"...perimeter..."

"Fuck me," Knocker growled and kept moving up the stairs.

When he reached the top, he directed two of the

security men to watch the stairwell. But no one came. No one armed, anyway.

Knocker looked at the gathering around the fallen president, his wife hunched over him. Cara came to his side. "Are you all right?"

"Been better. What happened?"

"Sniper."

"Shit." He looked up at the helicopter as it came in. "Only a few minutes more."

———

As soon as he'd taken the shot and saw Lopez go down, Forest called back his people. There was no point in losing anymore. Leave that up to the natives.

He retreated down to the street and regrouped with his people. Crypto Graph ran across to him and said, "You pulled us back too early, Trent. Team Reaper were there."

Forest frowned. "How do you know?"

"Remember the documents you gave us to study? I recognized the Brit. Jensen."

"It's too late now. We'll regroup and go from there. We accomplished our mission."

"Roger that."

"Don't worry, Crypto, we'll get Kane and the rest of his people."

As he looked up, he saw the Chinook lifting clear of the embassy roof. Their time would come.

———

Nelson looked at the television screen and shook his head. The ticker at the bottom told the story. President Francisco Lopez had been assassinated only moments before he was to board the helicopter which would get him out of the country. The British were screaming.

Coster opened the door to Nelson's office and walked in unannounced. He shut it behind him and stared at Nelson. "Good news, Richard. Venezuela has a new president and is now under martial law. Give it a few weeks and they'll be trading with the US, and we'll be lining our pockets with money."

"Damn it, Randall, he wasn't meant to be killed. Just imprisoned."

"He was about to escape. Trent did what needed to be done."

"Trent Forest?"

"That's right."

"Shit."

"He gets things done. Now we can concentrate on Sierra Leone."

"More bloodshed."

"Crack a few eggs and all that. I've sent word to Forest to relocate his people there as quickly as possible to support Jack Harding." Coster's eyes narrowed. "You're not getting cold feet are you, Richard?"

"No. But if the US is linked to any of this, there will be hell to pay with the international community."

"Then we'll make sure we're not."

Nelson nodded. "Fine, just so it isn't."

"You worry too much." Coster laughed and turned and walked out.

The president reached for the phone. Dialed and

waited for the voice. "There's something you should know."

———

TAIPEI, TAIWAN

"Welcome to Chinese Democracy," Borden Hunt said to Rucker as they stood looking at the half naked dancer gyrating against the chrome pole. "You can't tell me that the influence of the west is better for some places."

Rucker nodded. "Just the place our target likes to hang out."

"You see him?"

"No."

"Then let's ask around. Just be aware that this is a western bar, not a damn communist one. We fuck up here, someone will try to kill us."

Rucker smiled. "You've got to love it."

They worked their way through the club. Hunt went up to the bar and bought a drink. He showed a picture to the bar person, a young man with a permanent sneer. "You seen him?"

"Huh?"

"Him?" Hunt asked pointing at the picture.

The man shook his head. "No."

Meanwhile, Rucker was questioning one of the girls. A short Asian with small breasts, wearing nothing but a red sparkly thong. "Have you seen this guy?"

She shook her head vigorously. "No, no, no, no."

"Are you sure?"

She hurried away without speaking another word.

This went on for a few minutes before a tall woman approached him and said, "Come with me. I suck your dick."

"No, I don't want—"

"Come with, it be good."

Suddenly Rucker realized that there was something in her expression that gave him a hint there was more to her offer than he first thought. He nodded. "All right."

He looked around and caught Hunt's attention. The former SEAL team leader followed them at a distance as they disappeared up a stair well. Hunt was about to put his foot on the first step when two men appeared behind him. "Are you going somewhere, American?"

Hunt rolled his eyes before turning. The last thing he wanted was trouble. "Just going upstairs."

The two men grinned. Both wore suits, and from the bulges under their coats, they were armed. *Great. Taiwanese organized crime.*

"Maybe you better rethink that option," the bigger of the two said.

"I'm not allowed to go up there?"

He shook his head. "Not without a girl."

"Oh, right. I need a girl."

"That's right."

He looked around the room. "What about her?" he asked, pointing at a waitress.

"No."

Hunt found another. "Her?"

"No."

He was starting to build a picture.

"Maybe I'll go back to the bar and get a drink."

"Now you get the picture."

Hunt walked back to the bar and on the way, said in a low voice, "Rucker, something is happening up there. You're on your own."

"Copy."

————

"Who are you talking to?" the prostitute asked.

"Myself," Rucker lied. "I always do it."

"Come this way."

She directed him along a hallway and stopped outside a door at the end. "We go in here."

The woman opened it and Rucker stepped through. "Oh, shit."

Inside were seven men. Their target, another man dressed in a black suit, and what looked to be five bodyguards. One of them stepped forward and searched Rucker, relieving him of his weapon.

"This is him," the prostitute said. "The one who was asking questions."

"Thank you, Li-Jing," said the Asian man sitting opposite Russell Frost. On the table was an open briefcase with something electronic inside.

Frost leaned forward and closed it. "I will be leaving, Hao-Yu."

Hao-Yu?

The man nodded. "I will take care of things from here. Tell Mr. Coster that everything will be accomplished."

"Thank you." Frost stood up and shook hands with Yu. He looked at Rucker and said, "Good luck."

"Talk to me, buddy. What's going on?" Hunt said into Rucker's ear.

Li-Jing said, "There was another one. A man."

"I will have my men take care of it," Yu said.

Rucker looked around him and knew his situation was dire. He said to Frost, "Nice piece of kit."

"The Chinese won't think so when their planes start falling from the sky."

The former SEAL said, "So it sends an electronic pulse out and the planes just stop, is that it?"

"Something like that. It's like an EMP targeted at China's Next Gen fighters."

"So you just switch it on and bingo?"

"Not as simple as that. It needs to be logged into a Chinese military satellite which will enable it to send the signal out. The only way to do that is in China. Hence Mr. Yu and his friends. Once the war starts, it will be activated and China's air force will be useless."

"What about the PLA?"

"With the airpower the US will have in the region they won't even get near the coast. They will be forced to the negotiating table."

"Nelson is risking the lives of thousands on this plan working?" Rucker asked.

"Not Nelson. He's just a puppet. No, this is the brainchild of the new regime."

"What new regime?"

Frost smiled coldly. "The United Patriots of America. We're taking back our country."

"You get that, Bord?" Rucker asked.

"Sure did, Ruck."

"Go get them, buddy. Wish I could be with you."

"I'm sorry, kid."

"Damn you!" Frost exclaimed when he realized he'd been tricked. "Kill him."

Gunfire rattled and Rucker collapsed into a heap on the floor, a bloody mess. Just before he died, he hoped it wasn't all for nothing.

CHAPTER 9

TAIPEI, TAIWAN

HUNT HEARD the gunfire and knew it was all over for his friend. There would be time for grief later; right now, he had a mission to complete.

The SIG Sauer P226 came out with ease as the two organized crime heavies came towards him. He fired twice at the first one and put him down with two rounds to his chest. The second heavy was more difficult to hit because by then people were scrambling to get out of the way, inadvertently putting themselves between Hunt and his target.

He waited patiently for his line of sight to clear. As he did so the other shooter drew his own weapon and opened fire, regardless of the collateral damage.

The first round hit a patron, the second flew wide of Hunt; there was no third because the former SEAL had a split-second decision to make and he took it. He fired and the shooter fell to the stained floor beside his companion.

Hunt looked around for more threats. They came from the stairwell to which he'd been denied access. Three men wearing dark suits and brandishing compact submachine guns. The predicament he found himself in was becoming dire.

They opened fire immediately and a hailstorm of bullets found flesh and immovable objects. Patrons were cut down as though slashed by an invisible sword, buckling and then falling.

Hunt dived behind a lounge and felt the bullets impact it. He crawled along on his belly as rounds cut through the air above him. He heard the high-pitched shriek of a wounded girl piercing the gunfire.

Coming to his hands and knees, Hunt launched himself to his feet, running towards a thick column. He took shelter behind it as bullets peppered it, taking off chunks of wood.

Hunt returned fire, a couple of shots which found their mark, buried into the soft flesh of a shooter. He screeched in pain and staggered before sinking to his knees.

Not waiting for the angry reaction he knew was to come, Hunt ran towards the bar, firing as he went. At the last moment, the former SEAL launched himself across the polished countertop, taking half-filled glasses with him in a dive as graceful as an Olympian who got it all wrong.

The landing hurt. Hunt hit shoulder first on the hard floor and pain shot through his body. He grimaced and rolled onto his knees. Bullets hammered into the bottles and glasses on the shelves above, glass and alcohol showering him, forming a mosaic pattern on the floor around him.

Hunt came up and fired four hasty shots at the shooters. He missed with three but the fourth clipped one of the two remaining shooter's arms. The man reeled but remained upright as he tried to steady himself.

Hunt went to fire again but realized his gun was empty.

He dropped back down and reloaded the P226 before rejoining the fight. When he rose once more, this time he fired half the magazine. Eight rounds of the fifteen available. This time, however, both hostile shooters were down.

Hunt came to his feet and hurried towards the exit, putting two rounds into the squirming shooters as he went.

———

"Are we secure, sir?" Hunt asked.

"As we can be, Bord," Hank Jones replied. "What's your status?"

"We've got an eagle down, sir, and one on the run."

There was a moment of silence before Jones asked, "How bad are you compromised, Chief?"

"Blown sky high, sir." Hunt was taking shelter under an overpass, deep in the shadows. "We were able to gather some intel, sir, before it went to shit."

"Let's get you safe and then you can fill me in," Jones said.

"Negative, sir. Debrief now."

"All right, go."

"The HVT met with Hao-Yu. I assume he's the head of the Taiwanese Syndicate. He gave him a briefcase with some electronic device in it. It needs to connect to a Chinese satellite to be able to knock out their Next Gen fighters. To do that Yu has to take it to China. I need to get into the country if I'm going to stop him."

"I'll see what I can do."

"There was also mention of a new regime. The United Patriots of America. Apparently, Nelson is just a puppet."

"This is worse than we first thought. I need to kick this up to Whitehall. Listen carefully, I'll tell you where to go. Shelter in place until you hear from me. Understood?"

"Yes, sir."

————

MI6, LONDON

Jeremy West couldn't believe what he was hearing as Hank Jones laid out everything that they knew. Beside Jones was Frank Fitzgerald, the head of MI5. He, too, thought the idea of what was happening fanciful.

West shook his head. "You're telling me that a shadow government led by a Texas Senator is pushing the world towards war over Taiwan?"

"Yes," Jones said.

"And that there are components in their Next Gen planes that have the ability to bring them down when activated?"

"That's correct."

"Who has it?"

"Someone named Hao-Yu."

"This is very hard to believe, Hank," West said almost scornfully.

"I thought so too, sir, but I've had it verified by two sources. One I trust implicitly. He lost his partner getting this information, Jeremy."

"But why? What is the point?"

"I'm not sure. I think the ultimate goal would be to bring China and her economy to her knees, forcing them to have to rely on the US for everything."

Fitzgerald said, "They haven't thought it through very well, have they?"

"Why is that?"

"Well, China has the largest army in the world. Their fleet is more than capable, and even without their Next Gen fighters they still have all of their older beasts. Have they thought that they may go nuclear with their subs?"

"I doubt it. People like this only think one-dimensionally."

"Then there is the other problem," West added.

"What's that?"

"Over the past few years, we've been getting limited intel about the Chinese slipping sleepers into Taiwan."

"How many?" Jones asked.

"Maybe as many as ten thousand."

"You have got to be fucking kidding?" Jones hissed. "How are you the only ones to know this?"

"We shared it," West said. "And it was summarily dismissed."

"Christ. They could target anything they wanted to. Airforce, navy, nuclear facilities."

"That's right, so even if the Chinese are knocked out of the air, they have more than enough capability to bring Taiwan to its knees. All the Chinese government has been waiting for is an opportunity to enact their plan. If this goes ahead, then all bets are off. And if the President of the United States is in the country at the time, he will be a priority target."

"There has to be something we're missing here," Fitzgerald said. "Something doesn't add up."

Jones nodded. "Let's think about it. The shadow government draws the Chinese into a war. They launch their planes which promptly fall from the sky. They're not going to stop at that. The Chinese president will initiate their plan to bring Taiwan down from the inside."

"Not if he can't," West said.

"You mean take out the Chinese president somehow?" Jones asked.

"Yes."

"How would they get the opportunity to do that? He never goes anywhere."

"He does in the next couple of days," West said. "He's going to Sierra Leone to ink a deal with their president. It involves security, and their Belt and Road initiative."

"Oh, fuck it," Jones growled.

"What is it?" West asked.

"They're going to use the coup as cover to take out the Chinese president."

"The next in line will take over and initiate the plan," West pointed out.

They stared at each other. It was Fitzgerald who said what they were thinking. "What if the Chinese have a shadow government of their own?"

"Impossible!" West exploded.

"They would only need two or three at the top to make it work. The Premier of the State Council takes over and then they do as he says."

"There still has to be a response."

"Yes, a measured one. They send their troops across the strait, launch a few missiles, but with the limited air power they have, there is no hope of succeeding. The Chinese pull back, they get sanctioned by the U.N. but the US treats them with leniency and Taiwan becomes its own nation. China relies on the US for support. The US helps Taiwan rebuild any damaged infrastructure."

Jones said, "We need to look into the Chinese Premier."

"I can have my people do a deeper dive on him," West said. "Maybe take a couple of days. You do realize that if all this fantasy turns out to be reality, someone is going to have to stop it?"

Jones nodded. "That's what has me most concerned. I need to re-task my people."

———

DJIBOUTI

Mary Thurston gathered her team around her and relayed the news. "We're being re-tasked. Something has come up and we need to make sure that we accomplish our mission."

"Sounds important," Knocker said.

"As important as protecting the Chinese president."

Brick's eyebrows shot up. "Are you serious?"

"Very. It is believed that Xi Liu will be the target of an assassination attempt."

"Why can't we just tell the Chinese, ma'am?" Cara asked.

"Because we don't know who we can trust." Thurston went on to tell them everything she knew. "He must be kept safe, so, we act as overwatch."

"What about the arms shipment due in?"

"Secondary; we're trying to stop a war. I've got Slick digging into everything he can. Once I know more, I'll read you all in."

"I thought we were all done with this secret government shit," Knocker growled.

Kane said, "How does keeping him alive stop a war?"

"I don't know. We just follow orders."

"Sounds to me like we should just go after this Coster bloke and shoot him in the head," Knocker said. "War stopped."

Thurston nodded. "OK, let's just say that we did that, and word got out about a shadow government running the country. It would tear the country apart."

"So we need to do this on the quiet?" Knocker asked. "Someone should tell the prick who wants to start a war that."

"I don't have all the details yet; Hank is still waiting on some intel."

She dismissed them and waited for them to leave. Ferrero walked over to her and said, "This is fucked up, Mary. We're sending them into a hostile environment, which is about to explode, to make sure that the leader of the biggest threat to world peace is safe."

"That's about it in a nutshell."

"Shit."

MI6, LONDON—2 DAYS LATER

"It feels like we were here yesterday," Hank Jones said to West and Fitzgerald.

"It almost was," West said grimly. "I have news."

"From the scowl on your face it's bad."

He nodded. "It would seem that the Chinese Premier, Sun has a great dislike for Liu."

Jones shook his head. "This just gets fucking better."

West shook his head. "No, not yet; this does though. Nelson is going to Taiwan. I'm not sure what for. But the visit will take place in the window we expect everything to unfold."

Jones shook his head. "They're going to kill him too. If they succeed then Coster will be installed as president, and—"

"Wait, how can that be?" West asked.

Jones reached for his phone. He dialed a number and waited.

"Jones?"

"Yes, it's me, Nelson. Can you talk?"

"Yes."

"We think we've figured out the plan."

"We?"

"I'm here with Jack West and Frank Fitzgerald from the Security Services."

"Oh Christ."

"Just shut up and listen. The contingency plans Coster talked about. Have you heard any more?"

"No."

"Then brace yourself. We believe that they are going to assassinate the Chinese president and have their VP installed."

"What? How?" he sounded confused.

"MI6 have found the man has ambitions. We also have intel that you are traveling to Taiwan, is that correct?"

"Yes, it is on Coster's insistence."

"Is he still going to be on the ticket for the next election?"

There was silence.

"Nelson?"

"There has been a change of plans. Coster was elevated to VP three hours ago in a private ceremony. It will be announced in the next thirty minutes."

Jones swore. "Listen. Don't go to Taiwan."

"I—I have to go. I am to announce that there will be two new fighter wings stationed on Taiwan and to formally announce that the US recognizes Taiwan as an independent country."

"You can't. It—"

"I have to go."

"Before you do. Can I rely on you to turn this thing off if we succeed in our plan?"

"Yes."

The call disconnected.

"This just gets fucking better and better."

Welsh said, "He needs to be kept alive. Without him, it all goes to hell."

Jones's expression turned grim. "We're already there."

Fitzgerald shook his head. "If an author put this mess in a book the readers would castrate him for it."

"Don't you mean castigate?" Jones asked.

"Oh, no. They'd cut his bollocks off and make him eat them because you just can't make this shit up. Sometimes truth is really stranger than fiction. The question is, what now?"

Jones sighed. "I'm about to ask a man to die."

———

"I need you to do something, Bord, and I must stress that it is volunteer only," Jones said over the secure line. "You're the only man I think who'll be able to get it done. It'll save a lot of lives but most likely cost you yours."

"You don't have anyone else, do you?"

"No."

"Since you put it that way, General," Hunt said stoically. "What is it?"

"I need you to kill the Premier of the State Council of China. You need to kill Jian Sun."

PART TWO

THOSE ABOUT
TO DIE

CHAPTER 10

VICTORIA HARBOR, HONG KONG

THEY WERE Global Corporation's retrieval team. A specialist group inside a specialist organization. There were five of them. Three men, two women. The team commander was a man named Ian Groves, former major in the British Special Boat Service, commander of M Squadron. Now he commanded another elite team codenamed ODIN after the Norse god of war.

Groves was a big man with dark hair. Being a sound tactician and his experience in the SBS made him the perfect choice for commander.

The rest of his team consisted of Helen Smith, former soldier with the Royal Anglian Regiment, Rose Holden, descendant of a British father and Asian mother from Hong Kong, who'd been MI6, Paul Cross, another SBS recruit, and Evan Norris formerly of The Rifles Regiment. All now were ODIN.

"Ladies and gentlemen are we ready to execute on my order?" Groves asked with his typical British aplomb. He sounded like a British lord rather than a former soldier.

"Odin Two ready." Helen Smith.

"Odin Three ready." Cross.

"Odin Four ready." Norris.

And from beside him in the van, Rose Holden said, "Odin Five Ready."

Groves paused. This was always the tense moment. Right before they breached and secured a target.

Tonight, it was a young man named Qui Chen, a Hong Kong national that MI6 had recruited not long after the Hong Kong riots. He'd been sending them back intel through what was thought to be a secure system, when he'd been found out and picked up by agents for the Ministry of State Security.

Tomorrow he was to be transferred to the mainland where he would disappear into the system. Tonight was ODIN's only chance to get him out.

He was being kept in a warehouse on the water-front. Intel had at least eight X-rays onsite. Across the bay, sequestered on a wharf-side crane was Helen, armed with an Accuracy International Sniper rifle. From there she had a clear field of fire.

Norris and Cross would come out of the water and move across the open area in front of the warehouse then engage the guards within. They would secure the building and then extract the target to an awaiting van which Holden and Groves were in. They would then rendezvous with Smith at the boat where they would then extract from Hong Kong.

Provided everything went to plan.

Groves's voice came over the comms. "All elements, execute."

Cross came up over the edge of the wharf first and unslung the Heckler and Koch MP5SD from his shoulder. He crouched behind a large forty-foot container and waited for Norris to join him. Once they were together, Cross leaned around the container and stared at the two guards outside the entrance into the warehouse. "Odin Three and Four in position."

"Odin Two prepped."

"Send it."

"On the way."

The two ODIN operators heard the incoming round above them. As Cross watched, the first guard fell in a heap near the doorway. His comrade was only ten feet away and turned at the sound of his friend dying. But Smith was all over it and no sooner had he turned when a .338 caliber round put him down, too.

As soon as the last guard hit the concrete apron Smith came over the comms with a calm voice, "X-rays down, standing by."

That was the cue for the others to move, leaving behind their large puddles of water which dripped from them.

Cross led the way across the open area with Norris close behind. Their weapons were raised even though they knew that if another X-ray appeared, Smith would have them covered.

They reached the door and Cross checked it. It was open so he pushed it ajar, just far enough for him to see through it into the warehouse.

The building was full of crates and racks loaded with pallets of items. The ODIN operator slipped inside and took shelter behind a crate. He reached into his shoulder pack which they both carried. He took out a set of Night Vision goggles and put them on his head.

Beside him Norris did the same.

"Cut the power," Cross whispered.

Everything went black inside the building, and the former SBS man lowered his NVGs into place. "Let's go, Chuck," he said using Norris's nickname. "Work time."

Cross came clear of the crate and pressed forward, MP5 raised. In his ear he heard Holden say, "The HVT is in the right hand room at the back of the building."

"Copy."

The two ODIN men weaved in and out of the pallet stacks, moving like a well-oiled machine. Holden came back to them with a calm voice. "You've got two X-rays on your left when you come clear of the freight stacks."

As Cross came out into the open, he swept his weapon to the left. He saw the targets and fired two bursts. "X-rays down. Continuing."

"Odin Four, on your right."

Norris turned, saw, and fired. The Chinese guard grunted and collapsed to the floor.

"By my calculations, Odin Three, there are three guards left. Most likely in the room with the hostage."

"Copy."

They strode across the wide-open space until they reached the door they needed, where they paused. Cross reached for a flashbang. He looked at Norris. "Ready?"

"Do it."

Cross pulled the pin, opened the door, and threw

the flashbang inside. They waited for a brief time before the stun grenade detonated. Even before the sound had dissipated, Cross threw the door open, and Norris walked over the threshold.

All three remaining State Security personnel were there trying to shake off the effects of the flashbang. Norris opened fire, methodically picking his targets until they were all down. He moved towards the quivering man sitting on a chair.

"X-rays down, hostage secure."

"Roger that," said Groves. "Get him and get out. We're moving your way. Out."

————

SECURE LOCATION, HONG KONG

Numerous beer bottles clinked together as they toasted another successful mission. Groves couldn't have been prouder of his people. As far as assignments went, this was one of the better ones. Everyone did their part, and it went smoothly. Right at that time, Qui Chen was on his way back to Britain and to safety.

"We did good, tonight," his deputy, Helen Smith said.

"We did."

"What's next?"

"I don't know. Looks like there could be some down time."

His cell rang. At this time of night, it usually signified an occurrence of dire portent. He frowned. "Maybe I spoke too soon."

He answered. "Groves."

"Ian, Hank Jones."

"Yes, sir."

"I just received word that you successfully wrapped up your mission."

"Yes, sir."

"Good, good. Listen, I hate to do this to you, but I have another one of utmost importance."

Groves nodded. "I'm listening, sir."

Jones laid it all out and when he finished said, "It's volunteer only, Ian. Something like this I wouldn't just give it to you and say go. But you'd be an important part in a bigger machine."

"Yes, sir. I'll discuss it with the rest of the team and get back to you."

"I understand. Thank you."

The call disconnected and Groves looked at the others. "Listen up, we've been asked to do another mission. Volunteer only."

Cross looked at his boss. "Christ, it must be bad."

"What is it?" asked Smith.

"We've got to kidnap the President of the United States."

———

HEREFORD, ENGLAND

"We'll do it," Groves said over the secure line.

"I'll send you the details, Ian," Jones said. "I've still got to iron a few things out but once I do, I'll give you the rest. In the meantime, get to Taiwan."

"Yes, sir."

"And thanks, Ian, I know you didn't have to do it."

"Yes, we did, General. The major issue we face is the security."

"I'll see what I can do about it. Also, I'm not sure if this will help, but he likes his women."

"I'm sure we can work it. Thank you, General."

The call finished and Jones had another call to make. He dialed.

"Yes?"

"It's Hank Jones. I've got an operation in motion. You'll have to play your part."

"All right," Nelson replied. "What do you need me to do?"

"When my people come for you, there needs to be no secret service."

"How do you expect me to do that?"

"You're known for your philandering, so use that. It'll be organized from my end. I'll get you more details when they come. Don't screw it up, Nelson. Your life hangs on it just as much as my people."

———

FREETOWN, SIERRA LEONE

The apartment stank of stale food and something else he couldn't quite put their finger on. It was farther down on the same street as the hotel, but outside the cordon. Knocker swept the thoroughfare in search of threats before doubling back to the hotel. Outside the main entrance stood armed guards, both Chinese and those of the Sierra Leone Armed Forces.

Although not familiar with the conditions in the city, traffic seemed light on the street, maybe a sign of what was to come. They'd often found that the civilians were the ones that knew that shit was about to happen long before anyone else.

"What's the latest?" Cara asked Knocker as she entered the room, instantly screwing up her nose and shaking her head. "Man, this room is damn putrid."

"He's been here two hours and hasn't left the hotel," the Brit replied.

"Do you really expect him to? He's not due to do the signing until tomorrow."

Knocker grunted. "I was wondering about something." He pulled a map from his pack and smoothed it out on the table.

"Such as?"

"You notice how far it is from the hotel to the airport?"

"I hadn't spent a lot of time on it, but yes."

"If anything happens, then Xi Liu has a long way to go to get out."

Cara nodded. "You're right. He'd be a target all the way."

Knocker pointed at the map. "That means they'll more than likely hit him there."

Cara nodded. "Given half the chance."

Knocker turned and looked at her. "You want my opinion on this?"

"No."

"I do." They turned and saw Kane standing behind them in the room. "Tell me."

Knocker wasn't sure if the team leader was being sarcastic or not, even though the tension seemed to have waned. His head bobbed. "All right. Tonight. They're going to kick things off tonight. Liu will be evacuated, and they'll hit him along the route."

"It stands up, but what if they use a helicopter?"

"There is that possibility, but I'd say they'd have a plan for that."

Kane said, "What then?"

"Once the motorcade leaves, we follow and in the ensuing chaos, we sweep him up and initiate our exfil plan."

"Why not lift him from the hotel?" Cara asked.

"Too many variables. On the street it's shoot, grab, go."

Cara looked at Kane. "What do you think?"

"It might be the only way. I just wish we knew what they had planned."

Knocker swept the street with his binoculars. He stopped when he reached the battered van. "Ask and you shall receive."

"I don't like the sound of that," Cara said.

Kane nodded. "Neither do I."

The van was an old blue Mitsubishi, not unlike some Knocker had used for surveillance when he was in the Regiment. His guess would be that he'd find two former Special Forces operators inside monitoring the hotel just as he'd been doing.

He wore ragged clothes and a Yankees baseball cap pulled down low over his face as he walked along the sidewalk, approaching the vehicle from the rear. This too was parked outside the cordon which was guarded by more Sierra Leonean soldiers.

As Knocker drew closer, he stepped off the sidewalk and onto the street, remaining out of sight of the side mirrors. His target was the double doors at the rear of the van.

When he reached them, he held his breath, hoping that the handle wasn't jammed or locked, and that the door would open smoothly enough. With a hand clamped on his P226, Knocker tried it.

The door swung open with a screech which made the former SAS operator wince.

There were three inside. One in the back. He was the one that Knocker shot first with his suppressed handgun.

The man jerked and slumped sideways before he could even get his weapon out. Knocker then focused on the passenger. More room to move rather than the driver who had to contend with the steering wheel. The P226 centered and spat again. The passenger slumped, too.

The van rocked as the Brit rushed forward. The driver was trying to get his weapon around to aim at the intruder. It was but a futile gesture. Knocker was on top of him well before he could come close.

The Brit hit him hard.

And again.

And again.

The man was stunned, and his head lolled to one side. Knocker turned around and closed the rear doors of the van and then went back to the driver. Pulling him from the driver's seat and into the cargo space, Knocker zip-tied the man's hands, and began to question him.

"Who are you?" he asked.

"W—what?"

Knocker slapped him. "Come on, fuckface, get with the program. Who are you?"

"Jackson."

"Where you from, Jackson?"

"Minnesota."

"No, where are you from? Who sent you?"

"Fuck you."

The man was starting to gather himself. Knocker said, "Last chance before I start enhanced interrogation. Who sent you?"

"Fuck off."

"You were warned, mate," the Brit said and shot him in the leg with the P226. The man screeched but Knocker placed his hand firmly over his mouth. "I did tell you. Now, who do you work for?"

"Jack Harding."

"Good, now we're getting somewhere. That wasn't so hard. How many of you?"

"Thirty."

"Where?"

"Place north of the city."

"How many of you are in Freetown?"

"Only us."

"You checking out the Chinese president?" Knocker asked.

"Who?"

The Brit slammed his hand down on the man's wounded leg. He convulsed wildly, a scream trapped in his throat when Knocker jabbed him in the neck, cutting it off.

"Come on, mate, no time to fuck around. Both your friends are dead. If you want to join them just keep riding the bike you're on down this path. Now, the Chinese president?"

"Yes," he strangled the answer out.

"What's the plan?"

"The plan?" He hesitated then relented at the pain coursing through his leg. "Tonight the coup will start. He'll be taken from the hotel by car to his plane."

"Uh, huh, and who is waiting for him?"

"Trent Forest and his people. They are to kill him while his security detail standby."

"The detail are in on it?"

"Yes."

"Where?"

"I don't know, they didn't tell me."

"Thanks," Knocker said and shot him in the head.

———

"I guess we have to come up with a plan," Kane said after hearing Knocker's news.

"We need to get inside that hotel," Knocker replied.

"What happened with doing it enroute?" Cara asked.

"As the head shed says, the situation is always evolving."

"We can't storm it," Brick said.

Knocker sat there thinking. But it was Kane who came up with the plan. "The parking garage. We do it down there. All we have to do is get in."

"Leave that to me," said Knocker. "Getting into places is my specialty."

"Good grief," Cara groaned.

"Fine. I'll update Bravo."

Kane moved away from the group and took out the sat phone. When Thurston picked up, she said, "Tell me what you need."

"A ride out of here."

"No can do. As soon as the coup kicks off, the airspace over the country will be shut down. Get yourself some wheels and get out of the city."

"Shit."

"Never said it was going to be easy, Reaper. The best thing I can give you is drone support."

"One more thing. Trent Forest and his people are here."

"Another reason to be careful. Listen, things have heated up exponentially. This is a three-pronged operation. If any one of them fail, the whole house of cards comes tumbling down."

"What do you mean, ma'am?"

"The premier of China is part of the whole plan. Hank has sent Borden Hunt into China to kill him."

"Be fucked...that's a one-way ticket."

"He knows."

"Oh shit, poor Bord. What's the other part?"

"ODIN."

"Global's extraction team?"

"Yes. They've got to get the president out of Taiwan before this thing kicks off."

"Why not leave the bastard there to burn?" Kane growled.

"He's the only one who can stop this thing. If he dies, then the shadow government will rise to power and that will not be a good thing. Especially for you."

"All right. We'll do what we can."

"Whatever it takes, Reaper. We can't afford to lose this one."

"Yes, ma'am."

He disconnected and turned back to the others. "We're good to go tonight."

Knocker looked at Kane and grinned. The Team Reaper leader shook his head. "This can't be good."

"I have an idea."

"Oh, yes?"

"I need comms."

———

"Slick, my old mate, how's it hanging?" Knocker said in an overly cheerful tone.

"Don't tell me, Knocker, you want something."

"Just a small favor."

"Oh, God. All right, fire away."

"How good are you at hooking into cell phones?"

"Piece of cake. Why?"

"I need you to hook into one for me."

"Whose?" Swift asked cautiously.

From the expressions on Kane and Cara's faces they already knew what he was going to say. "The Chinese president's."

"Shit."

"You can't do it?" Knocker asked.

"I didn't say that...but shit, Knocker."

"If you can't do it, then..."

"Give me a few minutes."

Knocker grinned at Kane and Cara. The latter seemed perplexed. "What are you going to do?"

"I'm going to have a chat with our friend."

"I hope you know what you're doing."

"Can't hurt."

"Oh, God."

A few minutes later, Swift came back and said, "Get ready, magic has been achieved."

The ring tone came and then a voice. "Hello?"

"Mr. President?"

"Yes."

Knocker gave the others a wink and the thumbs up as though he was talking to some hot girl he'd just met. "Mr. President, you don't know me. My name is Raymond Jensen."

"Who? I'm hanging up. How did you get this number?"

"Please, wait. I'm—"

The call disconnected. "Fuck. Swift, get him back."

Ringing. "Stop calling me."

"Don't hang up, I'm trying to save your life."

Silence.

"Are you still there?"

"I'm here."

"Have you ever heard of the Global Corporation? Team Reaper?"

"I have."

"Mr. President, send your most trusted man outside along the street to a Mitsubishi van. Have him look inside. It will help you verify I am trying to help. Honestly, sir, we're trying to save your life. I'll call you back in ten minutes."

The call went dead, and Knocker looked at the others. Kane said, "Do you think it worked?"

"I guess time will tell."

Knocker called him back exactly ten minutes later. When Liu answered, the former SAS man said, "At least you answered, that's a start."

"Tell me what is happening, Mr. Jensen. Make it sound good or I will hang up again."

"There will be a coup tonight, Mr. President and while it is happening, you will be evacuated for your safety."

"That is standard procedure."

"Yes, but there are people within your government who are going to use that opportunity to try and kill you."

"Impossible. I have my security," Liu snorted.

"They are in on it, sir."

"Now I know you are lying."

"Sir, those men in the van were there to watch over you just in case something happened. I killed them earlier today. They are not a lie. I can't go into all the details at this minute but understand this, there are forces on your side and the American side who are driving the two countries towards conflict. The AWACS plane was just the start."

"We had nothing to do with that plane."

"I know, sir, but a lot of people out there don't believe that." Knocker paused. "You must believe me, Mr. President. Tonight there will be a coup and you will be killed before you can get to your plane."

"Why would anyone do this?" Liu demanded.

"Big ambitions, sir. Your premier has big ambitions."

After Knocker had finished the call, Kane asked him, "What now?"

"We find a way into that hotel."

––––––––

The laundry cart rattled as it was pushed over the carpet strip along the hallway. The laundry hand stopped outside the door of the room she had the key for and opened it. Then she pushed the cart in and closed the door behind her.

Removing the cover of the trolley she said into her comms, "Reaper One, we are in position."

"Roger."

Knocker climbed out of the laundry trolley with a concerned expression on his face. "Someone was fucking in them sheets."

"If you say so."

He bent back down and took their weapons out along with their body armor. He passed Cara her M6A2 and then found his. "I told you it would work."

"Why? Because it worked in the movies?" Cara said.

"That's right. Now all we have to do is wait. Once the call comes through that the coup is underway, we go and get our friend."

"The only reason we made it this far is because their security is bullshit."

"That, too," Knocker agreed and tossed Cara her clothes.

She stripped down to bra and panties and put on her jeans and shirt, before putting her body armor on.

They were on the floor below the Chinese president's suite. Cara had been right about the security; it was badly lacking. She wheeled Knocker past a roving patrol, and they never even blinked because she was white.

It was now dark outside, so the expected coup would start soon. Then they would go. Kane and Brick would enter the parking garage and would rendezvous inside. But for now, all they could do was wait.

———

"All Reaper elements, we're getting reports of Rebel forces moving into the city."

"Here we go," said Cara. "Time to go to work."

Knocker picked up his suppressed M6 and nodded. "Nobody lives forever."

"Reaper Two and Three, I'm getting increased chatter on the Chinese network. It looks like they're getting ready to move him."

"Copy, Bravo Four," Cara replied. "We're moving."

Knocker opened the door and checked the hallway. It was clear. "Let's go, boss."

They hurried towards the stairwell and opened the door. It made a squeaking sound which was so common with hotel doors. The stairwell was clear and with their weapons raised, they started climbing to the next floor.

Knocker paused at the door and said softly. "Ready?"

"Do it."

Knocker opened the door and let Cara through. There were two Chinese guards ten feet in front of her. The suppressed M6 fired and the first fell. Within a heartbeat Cara had changed her aim and the second man joined his friend on the carpeted floor.

Further along the hallway were more of the Chinese president's detail. Cara fired once more, sending a third guard to an inauspicious end. All in all, it was like a training drill on the range in Hereford. Aim and fire and by the time she was finished there were six down and the hallway was clear.

While she watched their six, Knocker put a small breaching charge on the door of the president's room. In their ears, Slick said, "There are three signatures inside the room."

"Done," Knocker said. "Fire in the hole."

They pressed themselves against the wall and Knocker blew the charge.

The sound of the blast filled the hallway and debris flew across the floor. Knocker moved into the room and saw the first of the guards loom in front of him. He stroked the trigger on his M6 and put him down.

Cara was close behind Knocker and swept the room until she found the second guard. His handgun was up ready to fire but he was too slow. Cara had him down in a flash.

Knocker moved deeper into the suite until he found the president. "Mr. President, are there any more security?"

"N—no."

"Good. Now we need to get you out of here. The coup has started, and we need to get across the city to a place where you can be extracted."

"How do I know I can trust you?" Liu stammered.

"It's a bit fucking late now. Just follow the lady and you'll be fine."

"Knocker, are you ready?"

"Yes, ma'am."

Cara nodded. "Reaper One, copy?"

"Roger, Reaper Two."

"We have the package and are moving to extract."

"Roger. Be aware you could have some company directly. A truck load of Rebels just turned up at the hotel and are infiltrating."

"How? They can't know we're here."

"Target of opportunity," Kane said. "I'd say they're looking for hostages. Meet you in the parking garage."

"Roger. Out." She turned to Knocker. "Did you get that?"

He grunted. "Life was never meant to be fucking easy."

Cara entered the stairwell and started down. They had gone two floors when they met two armed men coming up from below. Cara sighted, fired, sighted, and fired again. Blood splattered across the concrete wall of the stairwell as the two men fell to the stairs and slid to the landing below.

They pressed on, stepping over the corpses to go lower still. Behind Cara she heard the rattle of gunfire followed by the sound of Knocker's M6. A shout was followed by the sound of a body rolling down the stairs.

"That'll bring them like flies to shit," he growled.

And as if on cue, the door to the floor below flew open to reveal two more shooters.

Cara raised her weapon. "More of the bastards. Hang on, Mr. President, this might be a little bumpy."

————

The two security guards at the front gate into the underground garage were down and not moving. Kane looked into the parking structure and nodded grimly. "Well, we now know where some of them went."

As they made their way stealthily inside, loud voices began to bounce off the solid walls. As soon as Kane saw his first rebel, he fired the M6 and brought him down. A second appeared and Brick fired. Two shots, both found their target. "Where is the Chinese president's vehicle parked?" Kane asked Swift.

"The cameras tell me it's on the next level down. It's gated so you'll need a small breaching charge."

"Roger."

The two men hurried between the parked vehicles, weaving in and out. A rebel appeared four bays over and Kane shot him through the head. Suddenly the underground carpark was filled with the sound of gunfire.

The echoing noise was almost deafening. Kane and Brick moved towards it rather than away. They worked their way downward until the gate was in front of them. "Brick, you're up."

The former SEAL set the charge which disabled the lock with a pop. Kane said, "Just like a surgeon."

They rolled the gate back and proceeded to the scene of the firefight.

There were six rebels firing towards a vehicle. A shooter popped up from behind it and Kane saw that it was Knocker. Then he saw Cara behind another vehicle to the right.

Using hand signals Kane indicated to a rebel to their left. Brick nodded and took aim. Kane picked a second shooter. "Now."

They fired and the rebels fell, dropping from sight. Then an explosion rocked the parking garage and things got a whole lot worse.

———

Knocker was shoved into the vehicle he was sheltering behind by an invisible hand. The air exploded from his lungs as he sank to his knees. Heat washed over him from the exploding Ford two bays away.

"Stuff me," Knocker moaned. He looked sideways and saw Liu hunched over on his knees. Then he said into his comms, "Cara, are you alright?"

Bullets punched into the vehicle he was behind as he waited for a response.

"Cara, talk to me."

"I've been hit," came the reply. Her voice sounded distant.

"Shit, how bad?"

No answer.

"How bad, Reaper Two?"

Knocker dragged himself up to see another rebel pressing the advantage and coming towards him. He brought up the M6 and fired through the windows at the approaching man, who clutched at his throat as blood exploded from a ghastly wound.

Now on his feet, Knocker stepped out into the open, the heat from the burning Ford still evident. He opened fire, trying to find targets, not worrying about his own safety. Then his magazine ran dry.

"Ah, shit!"

Knocker dropped out the magazine and started to reload when a bullet hit him in the chest. The amor plating took the blow but the Brit still staggered and went down to his knees. Grinding his teeth against the pain, Knocker tried to finish reloading then realized he was in trouble. He was about to die and there was nothing he could do about it.

Until more gunfire erupted and the rebels began to fall.

"Bugger me," Knocker said with relief as he watched all the rebels go down.

Soon Kane and Brick appeared, and he said, "Cara is down."

"Where?" Kane asked, the concern evident on his face.

"Over the other side," the Brit said. "I'll secure the president."

Kane and Brick hurried across and found Cara laying on the concrete floor. She looked up at the man called Reaper and said, "That hurt."

"What happened?"

"Blast. Must have got me just right."

He helped her up and she wobbled. "Brick, look her over."

Kane went back across to Knocker who had the Chinese president. "Mr. President, my name is John Kane. We'll get you to a secure location before we get you out of the city, sir."

"I must say, this is very unusual, Mr. Kane. It could be considered kidnapping and an act of war."

"We're trying to stop one, sir. Now, if you'll come with us, we need to find some wheels." Kane looked at Knocker. "How about it?"

"I say we steal something inconspicuous."

"You're right. Let's get it done."

———

"Bravo, we have the package and we're coming out."

"Copy, Reaper One, you have the package."

The Range Rover exploded out of the underground parking garage and turned hard left on the street.

In the distance the dark skies already held an orange glow emanating from the fires. "Slick, you got your ears on good buddy?" Knocker asked in his worst American accent.

"Please don't do that?" Swift said.

"Don't like it?"

"Not one bit."

"I need a route to a safe haven for our friend here."

Swift said, "The Security Service has another safehouse about four klicks from where you are. They're expecting you, all you have to do is negotiate the roadblocks that seem to be popping up everywhere."

"Piece of piss, my friend."

"We'll see. Turn right, two-hundred meters ahead."

"Roger that."

Kane came on the comms. "Zero, do you have a sitrep for us?"

"It's not good, Reaper. The rebels are moving into the city from all sides. They are supported by mercenaries who we assume are Jack Harding's men. An SOS has gone out from the government to anyone who can help. From what we can gather, the Americans have yet to respond but we know how that will end. The Brits and the French are spinning up a QRF force of two battalions to be used as peacekeepers. They won't be on the ground for at least twenty-four hours. Until then you have two choices. Go to ground or get out of the city."

"What about Global, have they got anyone in the area?"

"I'll check, but I'm thinking not. If they have, I'll see if I can get them tasked to help out."

"Thanks, Zero. Reaper One, out."

———

Trent Forest was as mad as hell. Every time he had everything worked out, these bastards seemed to show up and shit on the plan. "Do we know where they're headed?"

"No, sir, all we have is them taking the Chinese president and escaping in an SUV."

"Then fucking find them so I can finish it once and for all."

"We'll do our best, sir."

The link terminated and Forest turned to the man next to him. "Fucking incompetence."

Edison nodded. "I've been tasked to help in any way I can, Trent. Right now, we're getting reports of the French and Brits mobilizing QRF. You have twenty-four hours to get this done. After that, shit hits the fan."

"If I can't find him, I can't damn well kill him, can I?"

"Just letting you know how it is. Vice President Coster is becoming concerned."

"If he's concerned tell him to get off his ass and do it himself."

"You know I won't do that."

"Then get the hell off my back."

CHAPTER 11

FREETOWN, SIERRA LEONE

"WE DIG IN HERE for the time being," Kane said as he looked out over the city.

Getting to the safehouse had been impossible as the whole place was locked down. So, they'd chosen a site on a hill within the city. Steep slopes with rundown housing on all sides. From this position they had a 360-degree view of Freetown and all that was happening. Including the multiple fires, explosions, and firefights which dotted the city.

Cara said, "Everyone check ammo. I want a report in fifteen minutes so I can relay it to Bravo."

Knocker stood looking out at the view. Kane moved in beside him. "We don't have enough of anything to hold off an attack. We need to get some more from somewhere."

"You know someone?"

"As a matter of fact, I do," the Brit replied. "There's

a whole warehouse of the stuff about twenty minutes' flight time from here."

"Great." There was sarcasm in Kane's voice.

"Give me the sat phone and I'll have it here within the hour."

He passed Knocker the sat phone and he dialed in a number. A British voice said, "This better be good because I'm sharing my bed with two lovely ladies and you're fucking interrupting."

"Georgie, me old mucker, how are they hanging?"

"Knocker? What the fuck do you want?"

"I need your help, Georgie. I'm in a bit of a fix."

"Oh, yeah. What do you need?" Georgie asked.

"Weapons, ammo, shit that goes bang."

"You've come to the right place, mate. I've got all that shit. When?"

"Within the next hour, all right?"

"Might be a bit tight, mate. Maybe two hours. Where are you?"

"Freetown."

"Fuck off." The call died.

"Bastard." Knocker dialed again.

"No, Knocker, not happening."

"You'll be paid well, mate. Top dollar. Listen, there's four of us, on a hill, and we're outgunned. We've got bad guys everywhere and you are our only hope."

"Christ. What do you bloody need?"

"Five point five-six ammo."

"How much?"

"Four-thousand rounds."

"Bloody hell," Georgie growled.

"Claymores if you've got any. Maybe twenty."

"Keep going."

"RPGs, grenades, shit like that."

"You going to war or something, mucker?" Georgie asked.

"Just trying to stay alive, Georgie."

"It's going to cost."

"I expect it to."

"All right, I'll have it there when I can. Tell me where you are."

Knocker gave him the coordinates and then signed off. He looked at Kane and said, "Let's hope he comes through."

———

The helicopter came ninety minutes after the call was made. It touched down and the crew on board helped the team unload. Kane ran over to the pilot and said, "You got room for a passenger on the way out?"

"You?" the pilot asked.

"No, another guy."

The pilot nodded. "Sure, why not? Get him on when we're unloaded."

Kane nodded. He ran into a block building where they had sequestered the Chinese President. "Sir, we're going to put you on the helicopter and get you out."

"Are you sure it's safe?"

"Safer than here."

"Then why don't you come?" Liu asked.

"Unfinished business," Kane replied thinking of Edison and Forest.

"You are a brave man, Mr. Kane."

"Just doing my job, sir. So I can save the world from a war it doesn't need."

"I wish others were as wise as you."

"Come with me, sir."

They walked outside just in time to see the helicopter blow up.

"Shit!" shouted Kane pushing Liu to the ground. He knelt over him with his M6A2. "Everyone, check in."

"It was an RPG, Reaper," Cara said. "I saw it come up the slope."

"Knocker, check in."

"The helo is fucked, Reaper. No one got out of that."

"Did everything get unloaded?"

"Most of it."

"Brick, you there?"

"I've got movement down the slope about fifty meters," Brick replied.

"Roger, on my way. Knocker, start putting the claymores out. Cara, I need you to reach out to Slick and get us an overview of what we're looking at."

"Copy."

"Copy."

Kane looked at Liu. "Sorry, sir, I need you to go back inside."

He nodded.

"I read once somewhere you served, is that true?"

"Yes."

Kane passed him his P226. "Just in case."

Liu disappeared back inside, and Kane moved to Brick's position.

———

"Bravo Four from Reaper Two, copy?"

"Copy, Reaper Two."

"Do you have us some eyes overhead?"

"We have a UAV in position, Reaper Two. Bravos One and Three are online and ready to assist."

"Bravo One, copy?"

"Read you Lima Charlie, Reaper Two."

"I need a sitrep, over. We just lost the helicopter we were going to evac the Chinese president on to an RPG."

"Roger that, we saw. Is everyone all right?"

"Roger. I need to know what you can see. What we're up against."

"We can see a build up to the southwest of your position, maybe twenty individuals."

Below Brick's position.

"There are also tangos to your south and north. We also have armored vehicles coming in on the west as well."

"Shit. What type?" Cara asked.

"A couple of T-72s and some OT-64 SKOTs."

"I hope you have some hard points on that UAV of yours," Cara said.

"Roger that. But probably not enough."

"Thanks, keep us updated. Out."

Cara changed her position to the west. Once there she used the scope on her M6. The movement was easy to pick up as the vehicles traveled towards the hill. They would find it hard to get up to team's position, but they still had their main guns. "Reaper, we've got a big fucking problem."

———

Knocker placed out the Claymores on the southwest first. He then moved over to the north and then the south, holding some back in case they needed to fill any gaps in their sparse line.

Next, he passed out the grenades and a sizable portion of the spare ammo. The RPGs had been on the helicopter when it had gone up. Better them than the ammo.

"Knocker, back over on the southwest side," came the order over the comms.

He worked his way back over and found Cara and Kane waiting for him. Kane pointed down the slope. "See what you make of that?"

The Brit brought up his weapon and looked down the slope in the direction Kane was pointing. At first it took a while. "I see the rebels. Looks like there are some white guys with them."

"Beyond that."

"All right, let's—fuck me. T-72s. Are they here for us?"

"We should assume so," Cara said.

"A bit of overkill, don't you think?" Knocker pointed out.

"Someone is making sure," Kane said.

"Yeah, I bet I know who that bastard is."

————

Forest was talking to the assault team's commanders. Upon arriving on site, he relieved the rebel leaders of their command and placed Harding's men in their positions. "Listen, we'll attack from the south and north simultaneously. I'll have the tanks give you support. Put enough shells on that hill and it'll keep their heads down. Kill everyone you find."

"What about the Chinese president?" a commander asked.

Trent stared hard at him. "Everyone."

"Roger that."

———

BEIJING, CHINA

Hunt was met at the airport by a woman. Her name was Mei Ling. She was shorter than Hunt, had thin, long dark hair, and spoke English fluently after spending most of her life in Hong Kong. That was where MI6 had picked her up and brought her into the fold. After intensive training, she had been released back into the wild as an agent in Beijing.

"Mr. Hunt?"

She surprised him by approaching on his blindside. She'd been trained well. He turned. "Yes."

"My name is Mei Ling. I'll be your guide for today."

Hunt nodded.

"Do you have any luggage?"

Hunt held up the carry bag he had in his hand. "Just this."

"Then we shall go."

She escorted him out and into a parking lot where they climbed into a Haval automobile. "Where are we going?" Hunt asked.

"I have a safe place for us. You will meet the others there."

Hunt was alarmed. "What others?"

"If you think you can do this alone, you are sorely mistaken. This will need more than just yourself if you are to succeed."

"What is our window?" Hunt asked.

"Two days. That will be when the American president will arrive in Taipan. Once he does, Sun will travel to Quanzhou where there is an underground bunker. There he is to meet Hao-Yu with the device that will be able to bring the Chinese fighters down."

"So we need to take them both out and destroy the box of tricks," Hunt said.

Mei Ling nodded. "Yes."

"It's getting easier by the minute."

———

There were three others at the safehouse. All were Chinese, all were MI6 converts. One was a PLA general.

"This is General Wang," Mei said to Hunt. "He knows all of the premier's movements and the route he will take to the bunker."

Hunt stared at the general. The man had to be in his early sixties. "Why are you doing this?"

"My allegiance is to China, not to the man who wishes to kill it. I will help you any way that I can."

Mei pointed to the others. "This is Jin and Sha. They can get you things that you need."

Hunt nodded. "Right now, I need to know everything you do. The route and where Hao-Yu is."

Twenty minutes later the briefing was over. Hunt looked at the map on the table and said, "If what you say is correct, Hao-Yu is under armed escort. Along with his box of tricks. So is the premier."

Mei nodded.

Hunt looked at Wang. "How far are you prepared to go to stop this?"

"As far as it takes," the general replied.

"I need you to get me into that bunker."

"Impossible," Mei said. "It is like a fortress."

"It is the only place that Sun, Hao-Yu, and the device will be all together. It is the only way to take them all out. Do it at the same time."

Wang nodded. "He is right. Even if we get the device and kill Hao-Yu, there is still the premier. If we miss him then he will still be in command. No, it has to be done altogether." Wang looked at Hunt. "I will get you in."

Hunt nodded then looked at Jin and Sha. "I need a bomb and an assault rifle."

"We can get the assault rifle, but the bomb? How big?"

"Big enough."

"It will take time."

"Time is something you don't have much of."

"We will get it."

"Thank you."

———

TAIPEI, TAIWAN

"We have two days to set this up and pull it off," Groves said to his people. "We will have help from the president, but we need to make him disappear."

"Sewers?" Cross asked. "A bunker somewhere?"

"A plane?" Helen Smith put forward. "Get him on it and out."

Groves shook his head. "No, something better than that. Sewers are no good because he'd be down there for days. A plane can be shot down."

"Submarine?" Holden suggested.

"We'd have to swim him to it."

"Not if we had one of those tourist subs," Norris said. "They use them around here to take people around the wrecks."

Groves looked thoughtful. "How many can they fit on it?"

"A dozen, maybe."

"Can you operate one?"

He smiled. "Did some underwater delivery work in the Boat Regiment."

"Fine, get me one. All we have to do is get him there. Go to work. I want to see a plan by tomorrow morning."

As the others went to work, ODIN's second in command, Helen Smith moved closer to her boss. "This is going to be unlike anything we've done before."

"I agree. It's going to be tricky. We're extracting the most powerful man in the world. If we fail, we'll be classed as kidnappers."

"Or be dead," Smith pointed out.

Groves nodded. "I need to reach out to Hank Jones to see if he can get us a sub."

Smith said, "I'll see if I can get us some transport and a plan of the hotel where the president will be staying. Let's pray this works out."

———

"Jones."

"Hank, Ian Groves, I need a favor."

"What can I do for you, Ian? Is everything all right?"

"So far. We arrived all right in Taiwan, but we need a top priority item for our extraction."

"Tell me and I'll see what I can do."

"We need a sub pick up from off the coast."

Jones went quiet for a drawn-out period. "I'll make a few calls and see what I can do. How do you plan on getting out to said sub?"

"That is a whole other story."

CHAPTER 12

FREETOWN, SIERRA LEONE

BUILDINGS on the hill were burning. Orange flames lit the night. Knocker felt blood running from the cut down his arm, and the stinging pain it emitted every time he moved and it opened up.

The tanks below were like the buildings, burning brightly in the dark, courtesy of Hellfire missiles from the UAV above.

Kane came out of the orange lit darkness. "How are you doing?"

"I'm good. The Claymores slowed them down."

Kane looked down the slope and saw the bodies strewn on the slope near some of the partly destroyed buildings. He looked at Knocker. "You should get Brick to check that arm."

"When I get time."

"Do it. Looks like you copped the worst of it."

"Would have overrun me if Cara hadn't helped."

Cara stood up from where she sat. Her face was

black with grime and there was a small cut on her cheek from stone chips. "We make a good team. How is the president?"

"Hanging in there," Kane replied.

Knocker said, "They won't come back up this way in a hurry. I'll bet my left nut they try the east side."

Kane nodded. "How many claymores do you have left?"

"Enough to do the job with some left over."

"Let's get them on the slope."

"Yeah."

Into his comms, Kane said, "Bravo Three, copy?"

"Copy, Reaper One," Teller replied.

"Can you do a scan to the east for us. We're guessing that they will attack up there next."

"Copy, wait one."

A few moments later Teller came back and said, "Looks like you're right, Reaper One. They're moving into position, and it looks like they're placing SKOTs in position as well."

"Copy. How are the other slopes looking?"

"Clear so far. It looks like they're going to throw everything at the eastern side."

"Copy, out."

Cara said, "Let's go take a look."

They hurried over to the east where Knocker was placing claymores twenty meters down the slope, an excellent choke point where the assaulters would have to funnel between the buildings to get to them. Cara frowned for a moment as she thought about the new intel. "I don't get it."

"What?"

"They're going to throw what they have up this

slope when another attack like the last would do them much better."

"All right, Lieutenant, what is your thinking?"

"I'm thinking that it could be a diversion for a much smaller force to come up behind us."

"Even if it is, we've still got to defend against the attack. Otherwise they'll roll right over us."

"I agree, but we still need to be prepared."

Kane nodded. "Yes, but which side?"

"What side had the most cover?"

"South side."

"Then they'll come up using the buildings for cover." A pause. "Bravo One, copy?"

"Roger."

"We need you to keep an eye on the south side slope. We're starting to think that maybe a small force will come up while we're up to our necks in tangos."

"Roger that. Will—"

Sudden machinegun fire from the SKOTs ripped up the slope towards the crest of the hill. "Here we go," Kane said, taking cover.

Knocker joined them. "Head over and take up position on the south side, Knocker. Keep an eye out for anything out of the ordinary. Cara seems to think this attack is a cover for something else."

"Copy." The Brit passed the clacker to Kane. "They're all set."

"Take care."

Knocker grinned. "Does that mean you love me again."

"Fuck off."

Knocker disappeared to the south.

"Brick, you still with us?" Kane asked.

"I'm here, boss."

"East side, now. Keep your head down, we're taking heavy fire."

"Roger that."

Kane and Cara moved into position behind a stone wall which offered them good cover. Cara took some grenades from her webbing and placed them at her feet before checking her weapon.

Bullets from the SKOTs' KPV heavy machine guns ripped into the slope and tore the night apart above them. However, with the tanks out of commission, it wasn't as bad as before.

Until the mortar rounds started coming in.

A plume of earth climbed into the air around twenty meters short of their position. First the thump then the crump, and shit was getting real once more. "Reaper, it's only a matter of time before they get lucky."

"Can you see them?"

Cara brought up her M6 and looked through the scope into the partial darkness. "Negative."

Kane said into his comms. "Bravo One, copy?"

"Roger, Reaper One."

"We've got incoming—" CRUMP! "Incoming mortar rounds. We can't pinpoint them. Need you to find and eliminate, over."

"I'll do my best. Out."

DJIBOUTI

Reynolds guided the joystick with her right hand, bringing the MQ-9 Reaper UAV back around. Beside her Teller looked at his screen, working the Reaper's camera as they tried to find the location of the mortars. Behind them stood Ferrero.

"Like finding a frigging needle in a haystack," he growled.

"Just got to know what to look for," Teller replied in an even voice as he zoomed the focus some more.

"How many Hellfires do you have left, Brooke?" Ferrero asked.

"Two."

"Time on target?"

"We're good until daylight."

"That's something I suppose."

"Got them," Teller said. "Getting the laser up and—target painted. All yours, Brooke."

"Firing."

———

FREETOWN, SIERRA LEONE

"Bravo to all callsigns, we have a bird in the air. Impact in three...two...one..."

BOOM!

The impact of the Hellfire missile at over 1,500 kilometers per hour and the resulting explosion was devastating. The sound rolled up the slope and spread out across the surrounding landscape. An orange ball of fire rose into the air, illuminating the area where the mortar was sited.

Cara's face was aglow with the flash before it receded. "Good hit, Bravo One."

The gunfire from the SKOTs stopped briefly before opening up again. Part of the wall to Kane's left took a solid hit and disappeared. Ahead of their position, some of the abandoned buildings had started to crumble under the heavy impacts. Kane said, "Bravo One, get rid of those damned SKOTs."

"On it."

Back in Djibouti the UAV team brought the two GBU-12 Paveway IIs online. Both were laser-guided weapons. Moments later Brooke's voice came back over Kane's comms. "Reaper One, you have a Paveway inbound. Keep your heads down."

Like the Hellfire, the impact of the laser-guided bomb was devastating, possibly even more so. It was followed by a second and the two SKOTs ceased to exist.

"Targets terminated," came Teller's voice over the comms.

"Roger that."

With the SKOTs down and the tanks and mortars gone, it was down to the foot soldiers of the rebel forces along with their mercenary helpers to pick up the attack. They took to their task with a vengeance.

———

WASHINGTON, DC

A select group of observers were watching events unfold thousands of miles away in a secure room. Randall Coster was growing angrier by the moment at the failure of the operation to assassinate the Chinese president. "Get me the British Prime Minister. These assholes are fucking up my operation."

"We can't really do that, sir," a man seated two rows back reminded him.

"Then tell whoever is in charge there to stop fucking around and kill that Chinese bastard."

"Yes, sir."

A large flare lit the screen. "What was that?" Coster demanded.

"The SKOTs blowing up, sir. Most likely from a bomb."

"Do they have air assets?"

"Yes, sir."

"Why wasn't I told?"

"We thought you knew after the tanks were knocked out."

"Christ. Get us a fucking plane in there and shoot whatever they have down," he ordered.

"Yes, sir."

Coster turned to a man seated beside him. "Is your team in Taiwan?"

"Yes," Jack Harding replied. "I picked all Asian Americans just like you wanted."

"Good. I want them to hit the hotel and kill the president just as we planned."

"Yes, sir."

"Wait," one of the other men in the room, said. "I

thought the plan was for Nelson to announce US support for Taiwan."

"Too much screwing around, Henry," Coster said. "The whole situation is fluid now. Especially with all the interference. We've deployed a special team to kill the president. We then blame it on the Chinese, and we have our war. There will be no announcement."

"If you say so, Randall."

"I sense doubt."

"Everything is so screwed up, Randall, that I doubt anyone knows which way is up. The plan changes on a regular basis...I don't know how you can keep up with it."

"The plan hasn't changed, Henry. We start a war, we bring down the Chinese fighters, the Chinese VP negotiates a peace deal."

"And we kill both presidents."

Coster nodded. "And we kill both presidents. However, it would be easier if we could kill that son of a bitch Liu while we have him cornered."

"Sir, we have no air assets currently in the area."

Coster turned and glared at the speaker. "Well, fucking get some."

"Yes, sir."

"Christ, do I have to do everything myself?"

———

LONDON, ENGLAND

"I'm sorry for the short notice, Hank, but it is urgent," Jeremy West explained to Jones.

"It usually is with things like this," Jones replied.

"The intel boffins have been picking up chatter to do with the current situation."

"I'm listening."

"First, I understand your people were able to extract Liu from his hotel. Is that correct."

Jones nodded. "At this moment they are on top of a hill in Freetown, surrounded, and awaiting relief."

"Good grief, I didn't know it was that bad."

"They're holding their own, and the package is safe."

"Yes, that's something I suppose. But the important thing is that Liu be kept alive at all costs."

"I'm aware of that, Jeremy."

"I'm sure you are. Now, about this chatter. It would seem that a team has been inserted into Taiwan with the special purpose of assassinating President Nelson. There will be no announcement."

"That is a huge change to their plan," Jones replied.

"It has to do with all the interference they are copping. If they can kill Nelson, then they get their war."

"Not necessarily."

"Oh, yes, dear chap. You see, the team they have dispatched are all Asian Americans. All the world will see is Chinese killing an American President on Taiwanese soil. Success is essential."

"Shit. Is the sub on its way?"

West nodded. "It will be there."

"I will let Groves know."

"Please do. Now, about your trapped team. Tell me everything."

———

FREETOWN, SIERRA LEONE

Kane emptied the last of his magazine into a charging rebel. The man went down in a heap but was replaced by another. "I'm out. Changing."

Cara changed her aim and shot the charging rebel. Then she pivoted again and shot another to her front.

"Grenade!" Brick shouted causing Kane and Cara to duck rapidly.

The fragmentation grenade exploded, showering them with dirt and grit. "Fuck it," Cara growled and rose, shooting the rebel who'd thrown it.

Kane, now with a fresh magazine in his M6, came back into the fight.

"Reaper One, sitrep, over?"

Kane said, "Sorry, General, no can do at this time."

"Roger that. Just letting you know that there is now some movement on the south side."

"Did you get that, Reaper Three?"

"I got it. Time to lift our skirts and dance."

"Just don't get shot."

"Roger that."

Two more rebels appeared, and Brick and Cara dispatched them. More explosions to their front as grenades fell short on the slope. Buildings were burning and the gunfire from the rebels increased.

Then came the call from Knocker. "Contact! Contact!

Kane looked at Cara. "Go. Give him some help."

She nodded and said into her comms, "Reaper Three, I'm on my way."

Then came the explosions as the claymores were detonated.

Cara charged across the crest of the hill and saw the carnage before her. Buildings were on fire and the cries of wounded punctuated the gunfire. The winks of muzzle flashes lit the shadows, and she knew immediately that she'd been wrong, they hadn't sent a small team at all. "Fuck!"

Bullets started to snap around her as she ran towards Knocker's position. She slid in beside him and shouted, "Are you alright?"

"Never better, ma'am." He fired at a shooter coming out of the dark near a fire. The man fell but not before firing a round from an M203 launcher from beneath his weapon. "Down!"

Knocker crashed into Cara, forcing her to the damp earth. The grenade round exploded close enough for them to feel the blast.

Covered in debris, they came back up and commenced firing again. Beside Cara, Knocker grunted, then cursed. Alarm raced through Cara. "Are you hit?"

"Maybe just a little."

"Where?"

He kept firing.

"Where are you hit, Knocker?"

"Left side."

"Bad?"

"Maybe."

"No, no, no. Not you, too."

"Keep, shooting, ma'am. It's all good."

"Are you sure?" she asked.

"Yeah, I'm sure," he replied, then he toppled over. *"Man Down!"*

———

When Kane heard the transmission come over the radio his heart fell. He shouted across to Brick, "Go. We'll fall back to the secondary position."

The former SEAL said into his comms, "On my way, Reaper Two."

Kane took two grenades and pulled their pins before throwing them down the slope. Then as they exploded, he was up and running back to the defensive position defined by a second wall. He leaped over it and crouched down as bullets hammered into it. "Cara, how is he?"

"I don't know. I think he could be gone."

Time stood still.

DJIBOUTI

What's happening?" Thurston asked Ferrero as she entered the operations room.

"Knocker is down hard, no report on his current condition," Ferrero replied. He suddenly became aware that the entire team was in the room with him, watching events unfold on the screens.

"Fuck, we have to get them out of there. Damn it."

Ferrero said, "Brooke, what munitions do you have left?"

"A Paveway and a Hellfire."

"Drop it on that frigging hill."

"Sir?"

"You heard me. Pick a target, there's plenty of them. Inform Reaper it's on its way. Danger close."

"Yes, sir. Reaper One, from Bravo One, copy?"

"I hear you, Bravo One."

"We're about to expend our remaining ordnance on your position, Reaper One. Tuck your head between your legs."

"Negative, Bravo One. Give me two mikes, we're relocating to the secondary defensive position."

"Roger, copy two mikes."

"Affirmative. Will radio when set."

"Roger, out."

Brooke looked across at Ferrero. He nodded. "Give him the time he needs. Just keep an eye on them."

"Yes, sir."

Thurston took Ferrero to one side. "I just got off the phone to Hank Jones. There's been some developments. There has been a team inserted into Taiwan to kill Nelson. Get this, they're all Asian Americans."

"They're making sure."

"Yes, they are. ODIN is already in country putting their plan into action."

"Let's hope they can make it work."

"Yes. Or we're losing people for nothing."

CHAPTER 13

FREETOWN, SIERRA LEONE

BRICK CARRIED Knocker to the fallback position with Cara covering his back. He lowered him onto the ground and took off his gear.

"How is he?" Kane asked.

"I'll tell you in a moment."

Kane said, "Bravo One, you are cleared hot."

Cara asked, "What's going on?"

"We've got incoming, danger close," he replied.

Brick examined Knocker, found the bullet hole and looked up at Kane. "There's no exit wound and he has internal bleeding."

"Straight up, Brick; what's the prognosis?"

The former SEAL shook his head. "He'll die if we don't get him out."

Things were grim.

"Zero, this is Reaper One, over."

"Copy, Reaper One."

"Zero, we have a Priority One evac. I say again, a Priority One evac, over."

"Copy, Reaper. Wait one."

Suddenly the hill was lit up by incoming ordnance, the final two on the UAV. The sound rolled across the city, and the hillside was lit up by the orange blasts. Cara said, "I don't know what we'll do if that doesn't slow them down."

"Reaper One, this is Zero. Unable to evac at this time. Stabilize in place, will update when I can. Out."

"You don't understand, Luis. He will die if we can't get him out."

"We're working on it, Reaper. Continue mission. Make sure Liu stays alive."

"Brick, you have to keep him alive."

"I'll do what I can."

Suddenly bullets started to ricochet around them. Kane whirled about while Cara opened fire with her M6. Shooters appeared all around them, the incoming fire getting heavier.

Behind them, Brick cried out in pain and slumped forward over Knocker, unmoving. Cara glanced at the pair and shouted in frustration. "Someone fucking help us!"

The sky above them seemed to be torn apart as an AH-64 Apache helicopter flew low, firing its M230 chain gun at the multiple targets below it. "Reaper One, this is Viper Six-Four, copy?" A woman's voice.

"Viper Six-Four, this is Reaper Two," Cara replied. "Copy Lima Charlie. Glad to see you, over."

"Roger, Reaper Two. Just keep your heads down for the moment, we'll take care of the situation. It might get a little loud though."

"Understood, Six-Four. Heads down."

For the next five minutes the Apache made multiple passes expending most of its ammunition. When the firing ceased, the hill top took on an eerie silence. "Reaper Two, copy?"

"Copy, Six-Four."

"Just checking to see that you're still alive down there. Just to let you know, a Chinook is on its way. Two mikes out, we'll give you cover until you're loaded and away. Good luck."

"Thank you, Six-Four. Reaper Two, out."

Cara looked over at Kane who was hunched over Brick. "How is he?"

For the first time that she'd known him, Kane looked helpless. "They're racing each other to see who can die first and I can't do a damn thing about it. Get the president."

Cara hurried off to get Liu and when she reached his safe position, she stopped dead. "You have got to be fucking kidding me."

————

WASHINGTON DC

"What happened?" Coster demanded.

"It's over, sir, they extracted the president."

"The hell it's over. It goes ahead as we planned. I want the team sent in tonight while Nelson is asleep in his hotel."

"I'll inform the team, Randall."

"Now, get me Sun. He must know what has happened."

A few moments later, Coster was talking to Sun.

"You assured me that this plan would work, Randall," he hissed over the phone.

"It will. I assure you. Everything will be fine. I have a contingency in place that will ensure that our countries will go to war."

"It better work."

"Just make sure you are in your bunker within the next five hours."

"I will leave shortly."

"Make sure you do."

———

BEIJING, CHINA

"We have to move now," Mei Ling said to Hunt. "Things have changed, and the premier is on the move."

"Sun is moving to the bunker now?"

"Yes."

The door opened and Jin and Sha entered, Jin carrying a briefcase. "We have what you need."

"Show me how it works," Hunt said.

Jin put it on the table. He flipped the latches to show the bomb inside. Closing it again and removing a key, he said, "You lock it with the key to arm it. Once it is armed you will have fifteen minutes to place it and get out."

"Is here a way to manually detonate it?" Hunt asked.

"Yes, depress the lock. You will have to press it hard or it will not work. It is a failsafe so that you cannot bump it and make it detonate."

"Good. I must go now."

"Wang will be here shortly to transport you," Mei Ling said. "Good luck."

He looked at the three of them. "Thank you for your help."

The door opened again, and Wang appeared wearing his uniform. In his hand he held a sheet of paper. He handed it to Hunt and said, "Study it. You will need to know it to get into the bunker."

Hunt looked down at the page. Plans.

"Once you are inside you will message me on my cell. I will then move the pieces so that you can reach the core."

"The core?"

"The operations room for the bunker. That is where Sun will be. You must get that far to kill him. And you must kill him before he can order the fighters in the air. If they get up and then he dies, there will be no stopping them attacking Taiwan."

"Then I'd better not fuck up."

"There is one more thing," Wang said. "Sun has just ordered the sleepers to standby."

Hunt's eyes narrowed. "What sleepers?"

"Ten-thousand sleepers who have been smuggled into Taiwan over a period of time. They have orders to attack anything vital to Taiwan's defense."

"But if he's ordered that to happen, then—"

"He plans on betraying his counterpart on the other side. He will not bring the planes down; they are going to attack Taiwan."

"Christ, we need to stop him. If that happens and when Coster realizes, he's just crazy enough to send this thing nuclear in a minute."

Mei Ling's cell buzzed. She looked at it and said, "Hao-Yu has just been arrested by Chinese military police."

Wang nodded. "We need to go."

———————

TAIPEI, TAIWAN

Groves looked at his watch. "The president touches down in an hour, tell me where we're at?"

Rose said, "The sub is in position off the coast. We have also acquired the tourist sub which will take us out."

"I reconned the sewer close to the hotel," Cross said, "and it's all good to go."

"The hotel?" asked Groves.

"Prepped and ready," Smith replied. "Everything is in place."

"Good. Secondary extract?"

"It's a work in progress," Norris said.

All eyes turned in his direction. "Explain," Groves said.

"Just a couple of hiccups getting it organized. But it'll be ready."

"Shit, Chuck, you're cutting it fine," Groves pointed out.

"Never fear, sir, I've got it covered."

"Christ."

Without looking up from her computer, Rose Holden said, "It looks like betrayal is the order of the day, Boss."

Groves stared at her. "Speak to me."

"A source from inside China has just come up with an interesting theory. The premier is about to betray his counterpart. There are—holy shit."

"Speak to me."

"Intel is pointing towards Sun activating the sleepers. We need to move now."

Groves reached into his pocket for his encrypted cell. He punched in a number and waited for the person on the other end to answer. "Yes?"

"President Nelson?"

"Yes."

"Things have just escalated, sir, you need to be ready as soon as you reach the hotel. You could abort but then we would be back to square one and no better off. You have to trust us to keep you safe so we can stop the threat. Understood?"

"Yes."

"Your security detail, are they Coster's people?"

"Yes."

"Will you be able to get rid of them?"

"No."

"Then we will have to take them down."

"I understand."

"Be ready."

"Yes, thank you. I will look into it when I get back to Washington."

———

DJIBOUTI

Thurston stared at the message she held in her hand

and shook her head. She turned to Rosanna Morales and asked, "Is there any way we can wake Liu up?"

"No."

"Damn it. What is the latest update on Brick and Knocker?"

"Both are stable but not out of the woods yet."

"Thank you."

Thurston turned to Ferrero. She held up the message and said, "It is expected that Sun is about to activate all of his sleepers in Taiwan."

"He is going to betray Coster?"

"Yes, it would seem so. Odin is moving now, as is Hunt. It would be easier if Liu was awake but that's not going to happen anytime soon. So for the moment, we sit and wait."

"It's not like we have an operational team," Ferrero pointed out.

"No. Have Carlos and Traynor prepped and ready to go at a moment's notice. I have a feeling we're going to need them."

"Yes, ma'am."

———

Cara examined herself in the mirror without her shirt on. Her torso was black and blue with multiple bruises from their previous mission. She shook her head. She'd been lucky, unlike Knocker and Brick. Their team had been on the verge of destruction and was now combat ineffective.

As she slid her shirt back on, the movement made her wince at the small bolts of pain which spasmed through her body. The door opened behind her, and Kane entered. He walked straight over to her and wrapped his arms around her waist. "Easy, I hurt," she told him.

"Me, too."

"How are the two boys?"

"No change. They're stable but still out to it. Doc Morales said they might wake them up in a couple of days."

She turned in his arms and stared into his eyes. "We were lucky, Reaper. We've lost so many friends. Axe, Alex Joseph, Ruggles, Striker, Rucker, Anvil, and now it looks like Borden Hunt is walking that one-way street."

Kane nodded but remained silent. Cara continued. "Have you thought about getting out now that you've got Melanie back?"

He nodded. "It had crossed my mind."

"And?"

"I don't think I'm ready to make that decision, yet. What about you? Do you want to be with your son?"

"Of course, I do."

"Then what's stopping you?"

"I don't know."

"You know, there might be an instructor's job going at Global."

"Are you trying to get rid of me, John Kane?"

"No, just letting you know there are other options."

"I'll think about it."

The door opened and Brooke Reynolds poked her head inside the door. "I hate to break up the party, but how would you like to get a crack at Trent Forest?"

Cara looked at Kane. "I guess we're not retiring just yet."

As the pair of operators walked past Reynolds, she stared at them. "Wait, who's retiring?"

———

"I'm sorry to do this to you after what you've been through," Thurston said, "but we have a lead on Trent Forest, and I thought you'd like to follow it up."

"There is one problem," Cara said. "We're down two."

"Not anymore," Carlos Arenas said as he walked into the briefing room with Pete Traynor.

"You're up to bat?" Kane asked them both.

"You didn't think we would let you go out alone, Amigo?"

Teller grinned. "I was getting bored sitting around with my thumb up my ass. Felt like getting shot at."

Kane nodded with a relieved grin. "All right, let's do this."

Thurston said, "We received word that Forest and his people are headed to Mexico."

"I'll bite," Cara said. "What is in Mexico?"

"One American shadow government."

"I'm confused," Kane said.

"MI6 have been tracking chatter and flights out of the States. It seems that ever since we started to turn up the heat, they've been getting nervous. In the past three days, five planes out of various cities have all flown to Saltillo. It looks as though Forest has been called home to act as a security force against the heavy cartel presence in the area."

"What about Coster?" Kane asked.

"He's in Washington waiting to take over a rudderless ship when the time comes. We expect that when it doesn't happen, then—"

"Wait. As soon as the president goes dark, he will assume power."

"That might well be true."

"Then Groves needs to remain in contact with the outside world."

"He'll be doing his best. But even so, Coster can say that the presidency is compromised, and take over anyway."

Swift entered the briefing room. "We have more problems."

"What?"

"The Saltillo retreat isn't the only one. There are three more."

"Where?"

"Brazil, Uganda, Lithuania."

"Shit," Thurston hissed.

The door opened again. Morales poked her head in. "President Liu is awake."

"At last, some good news. Let's get him live into China as soon as we can."

Swift shook his head. "No can do, ma'am. China has shut down all communications going in and out."

"Oh, fuck me."

Kane thought for a moment and said, "Doc, will it kill him if we put him on a plane?"

"I hate to ask why," Morales answered, a skeptical look on her face.

"Then don't."

———

"This would rate as one of the most harebrained ideas you have ever come up with," Thurston said to Kane.

"All we have to do is get to a functioning news television service and get some airtime."

"Inside China."

"I never said it was perfect."

Thurston looked at the other four in the room with her. "Luis?"

"It might be the only way. But to do it, we need to move now."

"Rosanna will have to go with you. I'll have Slick find the best place for you to accomplish your mission."

"Ahh—" Kane started.

"What is it?"

"I was hoping to take Slick with us just in case we have any technical issues."

She nodded. "All right. Carlos, go and see if he's found a place for the operation."

A few minutes later the pair returned. "Slick put his laptop down and said, "I have two locations. Well, one really. The first is on top of a Chinese military base."

"That'll do."

All heads turned to Kane. "You can't be serious?" Thurston said incredulously with a shake of her head.

"We can piggyback on their transmissions," he replied. "It makes sense."

Swift nodded. "It kind of does, ma'am."

"Where do you land a plane near a military base?" Thurston asked.

"There is a disused airbase not far from the target area in Western China."

"How long is the runway?"

"Twenty-five hundred meters."

"It might do. Give me a moment, I have to make a call."

She left the room, removing her encrypted cell from her pocket. Then she punched in a number and waited.

"Jones."

"We need the Co-32," she said matter-of-factly.

"It's still experimental, Mary," Jones replied.

"It's the only way." She went on to explain what they were facing.

"All right," he said with a sigh. "It'll be there as soon as possible. I'll organize mid-air refueling."

"Thanks, Hank."

Back in the briefing room the numbers had grown. Now everyone was there, including Morales the doctor. Thurston said, "All right, listen up. You have maybe four hours to get ready before your flight to China. You are expected to be on the ground there in under five hours from wheels up."

As the team members looked at each other, Kane asked, "What are we taking, a rocket ship?"

"The new Co-32 shall be your chariot this trip," she informed them.

"What is a Co-32?" Cara asked.

"It is an experimental aircraft comprised of a remodified Concorde. Global has been working on it for a while. It has mid-air refueling capability and can carry a certain amount of cargo. More importantly, it has stealth capability and it's fast. And fast is what we need right now."

"Sounds good to me," Kane replied with a grin.

"Also, you will be required to wear new body suits at all times."

"What suits?" Cara asked.

"They are made from Synoprathetic fabric which is just like wearing body armor without all the weight."

Traynor raised his eyebrows. "Material? Sounds to me that if you get shot, it's going to hurt like hell."

"It does," Thurston said. "So, don't get shot. Kit up, you're going to Western China."

CHAPTER 14

THE LAUNDRY TROLLEY rattled along the carpeted hallway, pushed by a woman in a maid's uniform of black pants and a white shirt. The president was escorted along the thoroughfare by four men, all armed and providing close protection. One of them stopped and said to the maid, "What are you doing on this floor?"

She pointed at the trolley. "I work."

"No, you get off this floor. Shoo."

"I work," the Asian woman said.

"The hell. Don't you damn well listen?"

The woman pointed at the room across the hall. "I clean."

"For crying—"

"Leave her," Nelson snapped. "It's not her fault."

The bodyguard glared at her and followed the president into his room.

The maid watched them go and then opened the door opposite with an electronic key and went inside.

"Well?" asked Groves.

"Only four but I would say there are more throughout the hotel," Rose Holden said.

Groves said into his comms. "Team Two, ready?"

"Ready, Boss," Cross replied.

"Wait for my order."

Groves picked his MP5SD up off the bed and checked it. Helen Smith did the same. All wore body armor. Rose sat at a small table inside the suite and started typing on the laptop. "Just say when, Boss."

"Do it."

"Cameras are down."

"All teams, go."

Cross and 'Chuck' Norris came down from the balcony above. As he went over the side on his abseil rope, he detonated two things. One was a low velocity charge that shattered the sliding glass door and the second was a tear gas bomb designed to confuse rather than incapacitate.

By the time the two ODIN operators hit the balcony it was starting to take effect. They disconnected and entered through the now missing door, glass crunching beneath their boots.

Norris fired the first shots. A bodyguard dropped to the floor and didn't move. On Norris's left, Cross took down a second guard.

The third and fourth were just as easy to eliminate.

A burst of suppressed gunfire and the room was cleared.

Norris moved forward to Nelson who was doubled over coughing. The ODIN operator took a mask from his belt and forced it over the president's face. "Here, keep it on."

Cross said, "Odin One, we have the package and are ready for extract."

"Roger, Odin Three. Meet you in the hallway."

"Come on, Mister President, it's time to go."

They ushered him out into the hallway where the door opposite was open. They pushed Nelson inside and Groves took his mask off. "Get him in the trolley."

Nelson climbed in and they put sheets on top of him. Just before he was covered, Groves said, "Keep quiet. Any noise and you've fucked it for all of us."

After Nelson was covered, Groves said to Rose. "Get him down to the garage."

"Wait," she said as an alarm went off on the laptop. "We've got incoming in the elevator and up the stairwell. One of those guards must have triggered some kind of distress beacon."

Groves thought for a moment. "All right, clear as we go. Whatever we do, Nelson is the mission."

"Roger that."

The ODIN boss uncovered Nelson. "Out."

The president climbed from the trolley. "Follow Rose. Do not leave her side."

"Y—yes."

Rose took out her Glock and held it down at her side. "Mister President, you place your fingers inside my waistband and don't let go."

Nelson did as she said and stayed close.

Groves said, "Chuck, on point. Let's do this."

Norris was first out into the hallway, followed by Groves. Rose brought Nelson behind her and then came Helen Smith with Cross bringing up the rear.

Ahead of Norris the elevator dinged. Three men ran out into the hallway. Norris had his MP5 up and aimed. Just before he fired, he stepped to the left, allowing Groves to move up beside him. They both fired and two guards fell to the carpeted floor. The remaining guard started to react but was too slow. Both Groves and Norris fired together, and he died beside his colleagues.

"The elevators," Groves said.

"It's a bloody kill box in there," Norris said. "Better off on the stairs with the bastards coming up at us."

"The roof," Rose said. "It's the only way."

"Fine," said Groves. "We go up."

Norris reached the elevator bank and hit the button. Moments later, the elevator behind them dinged and the door slid open. It was vacant and they all boarded it. Helen pressed the button, and the elevator began its ascent.

Groves said to Nelson, "What happened to your Secret Service detail?"

"They were changed out at the last minute," Nelson replied. "They didn't like it, but I get last say, and Coster was most insistent."

The ODIN boss nodded.

The elevator stopped and the door slid open. They made their way to the rooftop via the last lot of stairs. Before Norris opened the door to exit, he said, "Watch for X-rays on the roof as we go out."

Norris pushed the door open and went left while

behind him, Groves went right. As expected, there were four men on the rooftop. All were facing outwards, not expecting the threat to come from behind them. Even though the alarm had been raised.

Norris squeezed the trigger on his MP5. The rooftop watcher jerked under the bullet impacts before slumping over. His partner whirled, trying to get off a shot at the shooter coming up on his six.

He almost made it.

The burst of gunfire felled him in an untidy heap.

Meanwhile, Groves had taken care of the remaining two. He rejoined the others and looked at Rose. "What now, Rose?"

"We—"

BOOM!

They turned and looked out across the city, seeing the orange fireball rising above it from the large explosion. "Oh, shit," Groves, said. "It's started."

Another explosion rocked the darkening skyline, followed by another.

"Missiles?" Rose asked.

Cross shook his head. "No, bombs."

"You people need to get a look at this," Norris said, waving them to the edge of the hotel.

They all walked over and saw what he was looking at below. Three vehicles had pulled up and were disgorging armed men. "Sun has gone all out," Groves said.

"We need to get off this roof," Norris said with some urgency.

"According to plans there is a fire escape at the rear of the building," Rose told them.

They hurried across the rooftop, Nelson sticking with Rose. Cross was the first on scene and said, "Shit."

As they all stopped and looked down, Norris said, "Looks like someone forgot to tell the scousers who built this place about the fire escape."

"It's a good thing I have a backup then, isn't it?" Helen said.

Norris grinned. "Always knew you would, lass."

"You call me lass again, Chuck, and you'll be the first one off this fucking hotel."

Helen reached into her backpack and took out a rope. She tied it off and tested it before saying, "Who's taking the leap of faith?"

Norris stepped up, letting his MP5 hang by its strap. "I'm up. You kill me, Smith, and I'll never let you ogle me again."

She grinned at him. "Let me know when you're halfway so I can cut the rope."

"And that there is why I love you. See you at the bottom."

Nelson said, "I—I don't think I can do this."

"Sure you can," said Groves. "We'll put you on Crossy's back and he'll take you down. Helen, you go next, help Chuck secure the base."

"Yes, sir."

Meanwhile, Rose was helping Nelson become affixed to Cross's back. Using a spare rope, he was tied to the big man and Rose patted Cross on the shoulder. "All good, big boy?"

"Better than good, Rosey, darling."

"Just don't let go or I'll have to kick your ass."

"Yes, ma'am."

Two minutes later, Cross and Nelson were on their

way down. One minute after that, Groves and Rose were fighting for their lives atop the roof with Chinese sleepers flooding through the doorway.

Groves dropped to his knee and opened fire. Rose pulled her handgun and joined the battle. She said into her comms, "Paul, you need to shift your ass. We now have a situation."

"Yes, ma'am. Letting go."

"What?"

"Got you."

"Asshole," she replied, firing back at a shooter and seeing him fall.

Groves said, "Rosey, you're up."

"What about you, Boss?"

"I'll be right behind you."

"Roger that."

Rose followed her comrades over the side while Groves kept the attackers pinned down. This was the tricky, bit. Getting down without getting shot from above. He fired another burst and looked at the edge where the others had disappeared. He said, "Cover me while I'm coming down, Chuck."

"Ready when you are, Odin One."

Putting a pair of gloves on, Groves said, "On my way."

Then he ran towards the edge, diving over it.

————

Norris raised his weapon to his shoulder. "Here he comes."

At the last moment, as Groves came over the edge of the hotel rooftop, his right hand shot out and grabbed the rope. It arrested his momentum and he started to slide down by one arm.

"I wish he wouldn't do shit like that," Norris growled.

"Showing you up again, is he?" Rose asked with a sly grin.

"No, but one day he'll fucking miss and we'll be scraping him up with a damn egg flip."

Norris opened fire as a head poked over the edge of the rooftop. Bullets ricocheted off the concrete edge, blowing chips off it. Another appeared and Helen joined him. She said to Rose as she fired another fusillade, "Go with Paul. Get to the sewer."

"On it."

They disappeared into the night as Groves touched down. He brushed himself off, as cool as one could, and said, "That was exhilarating."

"That's one thing you could call it, Boss."

"Shall we go?"

"Let's, old chap, let's," Cross said with more than a little sarcasm.

"Tone, Mister Cross."

"Stupidity, Mister Groves."

"Boss, we have a problem," Rose said over the comms.

"What is it?" Groves asked.

"You'd best come take a look."

———

"Well, shit," Groves growled. "Wasn't expecting that."

"Can we move it?" Helen asked.

"Nope."

"Why would you park a fucking truck there?" Norris asked. "The front wheel is right on the cover."

"No use crying over it," Groves said. "Crossy, get us some transport."

"Will do."

They exited the alley and Cross ran out onto the street, pointing his weapon at an approaching cab. The driver hit the brakes and bailed out, running away from his ride. "That was easy."

"Hello, dickhead, how the frigging hell are we all going to fit in that?" Norris asked.

"You're right," came the reply. Then Cross stepped in front of an SUV.

"That's better," Norris growled as the driver fled.

"You two clowns finished fucking around?" Helen asked.

"Yes, ma'am."

Groves said, "Chuck, you drive. Cross, in the rear. Helen and Rose get to babysit our package."

In the distance the sound of another explosion rocked Taipei. Groves climbed in the front of the SUV and turned to Rose. "Get a satellite up, Rose. I want to know now if we need to change to secondary extract."

"Copy."

Norris stomped on the gas and the Mercedes charged forward. Behind them men appeared on the street and started firing. A bullet shattered the rear window, showering Cross with glass. "Fuck."

"Talk to me, Rosey," Norris said. "I have to know where I'm going."

"Shit has really gone off in the city," she replied.

"Rosey—"

"Secondary! Secondary!"

He swung hard right on the wheel of the SUV and almost immediately stood on the brakes. He stared out through the window of the vehicle and said, "Maybe not."

WASHINGTON DC

"What the damnation is going on?" Coster demanded from his secure operations room. Every one inside was handpicked by the shadow man and knew their place.

"Sun has double-crossed us," an advisor said. "He has activated the sleepers in Taiwan which we were warned about by the British."

"They were real?" Coster demanded.

"It would seem so."

"Shit. What are they doing?"

"Going after critical infrastructure."

"What about the president?"

"We can't reach the hotel."

Coster paused for a moment. "What else?"

"He has launched China's NextGen fighters which have taken out some of the Taiwanese Airforce on the ground. But they are starting to respond now."

"And our forces?"

"Washington has launched fighters to fly security over the fleet. We have two Virginia-Class submarines on station in the South China Sea. The *Sturgeon* and the *Amberjack*. Both have a full complement of Tomahawks aboard."

"What about something with ballistic missiles on it?"

"That was never an option, sir."

"Damn it, make it one."

"Sir, you don't want to start something you can't turn off. The Joint Chiefs are meeting. Tell them you want more ships and planes and troops in the area. However, I doubt there is much we can do with what has happened."

"The hell we can't. Start with all those little fucking islands they have set up. Target them with cruise missiles. Have our bombers finish them off. Have the *Amberjack* sail into their back fucking yard and hit their naval bases."

"Which ones, sir?"

"The biggest fucker they have,"

"Yes, sir."

"Well, you've got your war, Randall," Jack Harding said from the shadows of the room.

"Jack, give me some good frigging news."

"I was just talking to my people on the ground. Nelson has disappeared. Someone took him. They killed his bodyguards and left in the night."

"I cannot believe it. Are they looking for him?"

"Yes, and so are the Chinese."

"With a little luck they'll do the job for us."

Harding moved closer to whisper into Coster's ear. "You should leave, Randall. Just like the rest. Just in case."

"I can't leave," Coster hissed. "I'm in charge of the damn country."

"It's all unraveling. What if Nelson reaches out and reveals what is happening?"

"Then have your people stop him. Send Forest."

"Forest is in Mexico. Besides, I couldn't get more people in there even if I wanted to."

"Shit!"

————

TAIPEI, TAIWAN

"Are you going to back up, Chuck?" Groves asked quietly over the tick of the motor.

"I was thinking I might," Norris replied.

"Yes, please do."

The man standing twenty meters before them on the street brought up the RPG he held and sighted on their stolen SUV.

"Now would be good, Chuck." Groves's voice held a nervous edge.

"Yes, sir."

Norris stomped on the gas and the SUV shot backward. He swung on the wheel just as the RPG fired.

"Crap," Norris called out as the rocket propelled grenade seemed to pass just above them, all too close for comfort.

It exploded against a store front, shattering the glass, and blowing what was inside to hell and gone. Norris selected a forward gear and the wheels spun as it shot forward. It traveled fifty meters along the street before he turned down another alley. Circling the block, he came back out onto the street he'd tried before. Only this time, he was further along. "Talk to me, Rosey."

"Turn left up ahead, Chuck," she said not looking up from her computer.

Norris turned left and planted his foot again.

"Take the next—"

BOOM!

The building beside them seemed to explode in a ball of orange. By the time debris shot outward the SUV was past, but it was still buffeted by the blast wave.

"That was a missile," Cross called back over his shoulder.

"Things are escalating awfully quickly," Groves said.

Thunder rumbled overhead as three Taiwanese F-16s flew across the city. Suddenly one burst into a ball of flame and fell from the sky in a million pieces.

"Keep moving," Groves commanded.

"Turn right in 50 meters," Rose called from the back.

Norris made the turn and jammed on the brakes. Ahead of them was a roadblock made from a burning pile of rubbish. Sudden gunfire erupted and bullets punched into the sides of their SUV.

"Everybody out," Groves growled. "Cover your side. Rose, you've got the president again."

The team tumbled from the Mercedes and started returning fire. Muzzle flashes erupted from the buildings either side. Norris called out, "There's a doorway on my right. Follow me."

Firing as they went, the team made towards the open doorway. Bullets kicked up all around them, ricocheting off the asphalt. "Son of a bitch," Cross muttered. "This just keeps getting better, boss."

"Just shut up and keep moving before we all wind up dead."

Moments later, they were trapped inside a hard-ware store.

"Set up a defensive position," Groves said. "Rose, take the president to the rear of the building. Stay with him."

The store front window shattered under the weight of gunfire coming in. They took shelter behind shelves lined with paints and tools. Norris said, "I'll see if there's a way out the back."

Through the broken windows, Groves began to notice movement outside. He picked out at least six shooters with QBZ-191s. "They are sleepers," he said.

Cross opened fire with his MP5 and brought down a running figure. The ambush. A face planted in the middle of the street, his weapon clattering off to the side. "That stopped the prick."

Groves said, "We can't stay here. Chuck, how's the exit coming along?"

"I've got a rear door boss. It leads out into an alley."

"Right, we're coming to you. Everyone move."

They broke from cover, travelling fast towards the rear of the building. Rose and the president joined them. Nelson looked as though he was done in already. "How are you doing, Mister President?"

"Are we going to die?" he asked in fear.

Cross heard him and said, "We all die, mate. Just not tonight. Besides, you've got Rosey, taking care of you. She's fucking hardcore."

Nelson looked at Rose. "Ignore him, I'm a pussycat."

They cautiously went out into the alley, Norris on point. He turned left and they started towards the end.

Suddenly the point man stopped and went down on a knee. Groves stopped beside him. "What is it?"

"A sewer cover."

"Get it up. It's time to go below ground."

The two of them worked on it and a few moments later the lid was off. The stench from below wafted upward, causing them both to wrinkle their noses. "Are we sure about this?"

"Go," Groves said with finality. "Our chariot awaits."

CHAPTER 15

CHINA

"SUN HAS ACTIVATED the sleepers and is conducting airstrikes on Taiwan, trying to take out critical infrastructure," Wang told Hunt. "Now that it is dark, getting you in might work in our favor. There is a uniform in the back, a general. Get it on and keep your head down."

"Won't that be suspicious?" Hunt asked as he climbed over.

"They know me. I will take care of it."

The vehicle started forward again and pulled out onto the freeway. Military trucks and police cars drove in both directions. The whole of China was now on a war footing. Wang said, "Sun will address the people of China in five hours. We must get to him before then."

As they drove along the freeway, the night suddenly lit up with multiple explosions. "What's over there?" Hunt asked.

"Fujian Air Base," Wang replied.

"That looks like a cruise missile strike."

The cell in Wang's pocket rang. He answered it, talked for a while, and then disconnected all while driving at almost 140 KPH on the freeway. "You were right. The US has launched multiple cruise missile strikes against military targets."

"It could be worse. It could have been nuclear. How much further?"

"An hour."

"Put your foot down."

————

ABOARD THE CO-32

"How much longer?" Cara asked Kane.

"A couple more hours."

Cara turned the iPad she'd been looking at around. "The situation is getting worse. The sleepers are attacking infrastructure, the Chinese air force are knocking the Taiwanese planes out of the sky at an alarming rate, cruise missiles are falling on Chinese bases, and the US air force is about to launch their latest strike fighters from Washington."

"Have you heard anything about the other teams?"

"No. The blackout in China isn't helping."

Rosanna Morales approached them. Cara asked, "How is Liu doing?"

"He seems fine. Tired but that's to be expected. It goes with his headache."

The 32 lurched as it hit some turbulence. "I hate flying," Morales muttered. "I thought these things were extinct, anyway. Especially after that Air France flight."

"This one was brought back to life," Kane said. "I hear they have two more. All for fast deployment like this, and with stealth capabilities. The Co-33 and Co-34."

"Ladies and gentlemen, please take your seats, we're about to descend to two-hundred feet. Enjoy the scenery."

Rosanne suddenly looked alarmed. "Why do I feel like that is a bad thing?"

Kane looked at her and grinned. "Just don't look out the window."

"Thanks."

———

UGANDA, AFRICA

What was late night in China, was around sunset in Uganda. Once the news of the shadow government's split, Hank Jones had activated Global's strike teams. Anaconda, Mamba, and Viper. Mamba was already in Africa so had been re-tasked to Uganda. Anaconda was in Brazil training BOPE, the military police elite troop battalion. That left Viper, who were still airborne on their way to Lithuania. Time to target, thirty minutes.

The compound that Mamba team was approaching sat atop the high hill overlooking a deep green valley below. They were traversing a gully which would bring them around to the rear of the compound.

"Mamba Two, hold," Mamba Three said from on point.

"What is it, Mucker?" Wood asked Cooper from twenty meters back.

"I've got a trip wire."

"Coming up."

Ten meters back in the four-man column, Mamba One, Jack Harris, Strike Team Mamba's leader asked, "What's the holdup?"

"Trip wire."

"Deal with it and keep moving."

"That's what we're about to do, Boss."

The briefing had come through while they had been in the Democratic Republic of Congo, operating alongside an SAS team. There were two targets. Ken Henderson and Lionel Brain. It was a capture or kill mission. Jones had said it didn't matter which. The two men were protected by a dozen operators from Harding's private security firm. Wood reached Cooper on point. "What's it attached to?"

"Frag."

"Cut it."

"Roger."

While Cooper worked, Wood stepped over the wire and surveyed the area through the sights of his M6A2. "We need to get moving so we're in position when the sun is gone," Wood said.

"I'm done here."

"I'll take point."

Mamba team kept moving until they were in position. The compound had once been part of a wildlife sanctuary, and in the distance, the team heard the deep-throated roar of a male lion. "Just as long as you stay right where you are, mate," Gerald 'Mountain' Hill growled.

He was the team's SAW man and his machinegun, like the team's other weapons, was suppressed.

Jack Harris and Wood crept up a slope and used night vision binoculars to scout the perimeter on their side. "I have two X-rays," Wood said.

"Affirmative," replied his boss. Harris said into his comms, "Mamba One to Falcon One, copy?"

"Got you, Mamba One."

Falcon One was the Forward Control Aircraft which helped the team on the ground with their ISR. Harris said, "I need real time updates on what you can see. Mamba Team going hot."

"Turn on strobes and cameras, Mamba One."

Harris reached up to his ballistic helmet and said, "All callsigns, activate strobes and cameras."

A few moments later, the team's strobes were flashing and clearly seen on the screen in the aircraft above. "We have four friendlies, Mamba One. You are cleared to go. Good luck."

"Copy."

Hill and Cooper moved in beside the other two. Harris said, "Woody, X-ray One, I've got Two."

"Copy, Boss."

They brought the M6s up to their shoulders and sighted on their targets. In a low voice, Harris said, "Three...two...one...execute."

Both weapons fired at the same time, punching back into their shoulders. The two guards dropped where they stood, never to move again.

All four operators came to their feet and started to press forward. Each covered their own area.

"X-ray at ten o'clock."

Cooper turned slightly and put the target down.

"Another at twelve, by the pool."

Wood took care of that one.

"Two X-rays coming around the side of the house at one o'clock."

The suppressed SAW in Hill's hands came to life and chopped the two guards down.

"Freeze!"

The four of them stopped and took a knee.

"X-ray on the rooftop."

Harris brought up his M6 and swept the roof of the main building until he found his target. He squeezed the trigger and the X-ray disappeared immediately.

"Clear."

They came up and pressed forward once again. Only moments had elapsed and five men were dead.

The Mamba team swept past the pool, across sand-stone pavers. Wood stepped over the dead guard by the pool and stopped against the wall by a large, double-glazed window spanning rooftop to the ground. Hill stopped behind him while Harris and Cooper had disappeared around the other side of the house, working their way to the front.

Wood placed a small breaching charge on the window and waited. Then, moments later came, "Mamba One, ready to breach."

"Copy. Three...two...one...execute."

The small charge on the window detonated and the glass fell like rain to the ground outside and the floor within. Meanwhile, around the front, Harris and Cooper made entry.

Wood's M6 came up as he stepped through the cavernous opening. A guard appeared and Wood fired. The man jerked with the bullet strikes and fell to the floor in the large study. "X-ray down in the study."

"X-ray down in the entry," Harris said.

Wood paused at the doorway. "Falcon-One, sitrep."

"You have two X-rays in the living room, one in the kitchen."

"Copy. Mamba Two is taking the living room."

"Roger, Mamba One and Three will take the kitchen."

"All callsigns, there are two X-rays in a room at the other end of the house. Believe they are your targets."

"Copy, Falcon One."

Clearing the remaining shooters from the house took another minute. From there they moved to the designated target area and made entry to the room containing the two HVTs. Moments later the call came over the net. "Falcon One, this is Mamba One, we have targets in custody, awaiting extract, over."

"Roger, Mamba One, extract is inbound. Well done."

———

BRAZIL, SOUTH AMERICA

Brazil was a different operation. It was the middle of the day there and the teams had been coordinated for simultaneous hits. But the Lithuania team was running late. Not Anaconda, however.

The two high profile targets in Campinas were a real estate mogul and a mining magnate. Both had funneled a lot of money into resources behind Randall Coster but now had runout when things were on the slide. But they hadn't reckoned on Global.

Team Anaconda was made up entirely of former British Commandos. Each had known the other in the service, and were a good fit when they came together with the formation of the strike teams.

They were currently staked out in a battered Mitsubishi van, one hundred meters along the street from the apartment block where their targets were. Unlike those in Uganda, these two, Hollister and Francis, decided to try the low-key approach.

Not always easy when you have determined people looking for you.

The Anaconda team was led by Dick Thompson, his second was a man called Stan 'Buck' Rogers. Operators Three and Four were Jerry Lewis and Les Cox.

They pulled on masks with skulls crudely painted on them to give them a gangster vibe. Each was armed with AK-47s and under their clothes they wore Synoprathetic suits. They had nothing to identify them on their person.

"Angel One, I need a sitrep, over," Thompson said into his comms.

Overhead was a Reaper UAV sending real-time feed back to the British Embassy where the basement operations room served as the team's intel base.

"Targets are located on the fourth floor, west side. Unsure of what guards are in there; we are seeing maybe thirty heat signatures inside the building. We are unsure who is who."

"Copy."

Thompson looked at the rest of his team. "Well, there it is. The order is kill or capture. With what we know, operating in broad daylight, I say we forget the capture. What do you say?"

They all agreed.

"Let's move."

The doors on the van came open and Anaconda moved. They ran across the street and into the building. Inside the foyer they met a young woman on the way out. Pointing his weapon at her head, Thompson said in Portuguese, "Don't move. Get on your knees."

With a terrified look on her face, but moving briskly, she dropped her handbag and kneeled as ordered. Cox moved in swiftly and zip-tied her hands behind her back. She looked up at him, tears in her eyes, and he held a finger to his lips. "Be quiet, girl."

They started up the stairs and reached the first floor. That was where their problems began. To get to the second floor, they had to traverse the floor and move up the opposite stairwell because the other was blocked off. "That stuffed that. What kind of fucking scouser built this joint?" Lewis growled.

"Get moving," Thompson said.

As they walked along the carpeted hallway, each man expected a doorway to spring open in front of them. Their fingers were on their triggers; only a slight change in pressure and they would fire.

The team had almost made it when a door close to the end opened. Buck's weapon came around and he almost fired at a five-year-old kid peering out through the crack in the door. "Fuck," he hissed.

The words had barely escaped his lips when a man appeared in the stairwell doorway. Their eyes met and the man flinched.

His right hand dived for the weapon tucked into his pants. The AK in Buck's hands crashed and the man was blown backward.

Behind him, Buck heard Thompson say, "Angel One, we're compromised. Moving to target."

"Copy, Anaconda One."

"Buck, get us up there."

Buck Rogers moved faster now, not slowing for anything. By the time he'd reached the floor required, there were three more shooters on the stairs, all dead.

He kicked open the door to the floor and was met with a heavy fusillade of gunfire, bullets punching into the wall behind him as they cracked past his head.

Buck took cover, pressing himself against the wall. He paused there for a moment and then leaned around and fired.

The shooter fell back, two rounds hammering into his chest.

Behind him, Cox said, "I got this, Mucker. He stepped into the hallway and moved forward. When he reached the apartment, he placed a breaching charge on the door. He took cover with the others and said, "Geronimo."

Thompson stared at him. "Dickhead."

The last part of the word was drowned out as the charge detonated and blew the door in. Thompson was the first man through—and the first man down.

Bullets hammered into his chest, stopping him in his tracks. Falling to his knees, his time was up as one final shot punched into Thompson's head, killing him instantly.

"Jesus Christ!" Rogers exclaimed and opened fire. "Where the fuck did he come from?"

The shooter within died before having time to fire any more rounds. Rogers moved further into the apartment and saw one of the targets, standing near a sofa. Rogers didn't hesitate and shot him in the head.

Behind him, Lewis moved left and opened the door

of another room. Gunshots sounded and the last of the targets was down. Rogers turned to Lewis. "You and Les get the boss up. We're not leaving him."

"Copy that."

"Angel One, this is Anaconda Two. We've got a priority four casualty, I say again, a priority four."

"Copy, Anaconda Two. Target status?"

"Targets are down. We're extracting with our KIA."

"Roger that. Good work. Out."

Rogers looked at Thompson. He was certain that the outcome wasn't worth the cost. "Yeah, out."

LITHUANIA

"A castle on an island, in the middle of a frigging lake," Viper team leader, Mark Howard scowled. "Get that drone up before we lose all light."

The big blond-headed operator was keenly aware of the pressure they were under due to the delay in their flight. But he had improvised, and they'd parachuted into the forest to the west of the target. It had been dangerous, but they had pulled it off.

The only way out to the target was the narrow bridge which was around a hundred meters in length.

The team of Howard, Welsh, Holland, and Sellens had taken up positions at the edge of a wood where which gave them a full field of vision at their target. A medieval castle providing sanctuary to their three targets: Pullen, Waller, and Allen. Two were bankers, the other an accountant. All three were responsible for the shadow government's finances.

Viper was under strict instructions to take all three alive.

Beside Howard, his second in command, Tippy Welsh took out a small Black Hornet Nano UAV and readied it. Once it was set, she turned to her commander. "Ready to launch, Boss."

"Get it out there."

The dark-haired operator had a sleeve of tattoos on her right arm, and they rippled as she launched the drone and began to fly it towards the target. The 6x1 inch UAV looked like a miniature helicopter. It had a range of almost two kilometers and could stay up for up to twenty minutes.

Tippy guided it across the water towards the castle. She picked up the first guard fifty meters out. Like a knight walking the catwalk, a uniformed shooter prowled the perimeter.

The castle itself was surrounded by tall trees so she'd been lucky to pick him up. She deviated the Hornet's course and elevation, and as it skimmed the treetops, she picked up another.

After a further ten minutes of flight time, they had pinpointed every guard within the perimeter of the castle. Tippy flew the drone back and caught it deftly in her left hand. Howard nodded with satisfaction. "Time to get wet."

"Fuck I hate water," Vic Sellens stated.

"Then why did you join the SBS?" John Holland asked.

"Because the SAS were all wankers," he replied having a shot at his friend.

In the time that the drone had been doing its recon,

the sky had grown darker. They slid into the water, staying close to the bridge, using it for cover. By the time they reached the other side, it was totally dark, and they could use that to their advantage. The outside of the castle was illuminated by floodlights brightening the night. Two guards stood at an arched gate which appeared to be the only access point for everyone to pass through.

Howard and Tippy rose up high enough in the water and aimed their SIG MCX Spear assault rifles at the two guards and squeezed the triggers.

Both guards fell to the gravel and died without making a sound.

The team climbed out of the water and paused. Howard said, "Peregrine One, this is Viper One, sitrep?"

"Copy, Viper One. Path is clear at this time."

"Copy. Tippy, lead out."

Tippy came to her feet and moved towards the arched entry. She paused and peered around the corner of the block archway and saw a guard standing near a black SUV. She was, however, unable to take him without alarming the other guard in the turret to the east. She waited until Sellens reached her. "Turret to the east, Vic."

Tippy went down onto her knee, while Sellens stood above her. Both picked their targets and then Tippy said, "Now."

Both Viper operators fired their weapons and the two targets died. "X-rays down."

"Move out," Howard said.

Tippy led them through the archway and into the courtyard beyond. Behind her, Holland and Sellens kept their eyes high, just in case. Howard watched their six.

Holland fired. "X-ray down."

"Contact right," Sellens said in a calm voice and fired.

The large castle door opened, and a shooter appeared. Tippy said, "Contact front."

Her MCX fired and the man dropped. There was, however, a shooter behind him, who brought his weapon rattling to life.

"Fuck," Tippy snarled. She fired once more, and the shooter dropped beside his friend.

Tippy took the stairs two at a time until she reached a landing and sidestepped just in time as a fusillade from inside exploded through the opening. "Angel One, check for runners."

"All clear so far, Viper Two."

Behind Tippy, Howard took out a flashbang stun grenade. He pulled the pin and tossed it through the opening.

The stun grenade detonated and Tippy moved into the light thrown by the massive chandelier hanging above. She saw the shooter staggering from the concussive blast, and shot him twice in the chest. He fell, and she shot him again.

"Angel One, we're inside."

"Targets are believed to be on the second floor, Viper Two."

She started up the stairs. They were wide, lined by a dark wooden balustrade on each side. Another shooter appeared at the head of the stairs. Tippy didn't hesitate and shot him, too.

Once on the landing, Tippy paused again. "Which way, Angel One?"

"Go right. Second room on your left."

She moved once again, working her way along the hallway with solid block walls. She stopped outside the room and stepped to one side.

The team used hand signals and Howard stepped up, pulling a stun grenade. Behind him, Holland unlimbered a tactical shotgun which took non-lethal beanbag rounds. Howard opened the door and threw the grenade through the opening. It detonated and the Viper commander thrust the door all the way open.

Holland walked through, the shotgun up at his shoulder. It crashed once and the first of the HVTs went down, writhing in pain. Behind Holland came Tippy who saw the threat and eliminated the standing guard.

Meanwhile, Holland took the second HVT down and then the others secured the room. Howard said into his comms, "Angel One, HVTs, secure; send in the bird."

"Copy, bird inbound."

Holland looked at the others in the room. "Well done, team."

CHAPTER 16

CHINA

THEY PULLED up in the lot and Wang turned to Hunt who was still in the rear seat dressed in the general's uniform. "This is going to be almost impossible," Wang said, looking at the security surrounding the bunker entrance.

"Listen, if something goes wrong, we need to do our best to get this bomb to Sun so we can complete the mission."

Wang nodded. He stared at the security who were checking everyone and everything going inside. "This isn't going to work."

"What do you mean?"

"They will find the bomb and it will all be over."

Hunt stared at the guards. There were four of them. There was only one thing for it. "Hard ingress."

"What?"

"I will clear a path for you. Once you're in the bunker, detonate the bomb."

"You know what that means," Wang said.

"I do." Hunt's face was grim.

"Are you sure?" Wang asked.

"As sure as I ever was. I promised a friend his death wouldn't be in vain."

"Then let's do it."

Hunt checked the gun in his hand. Once the guards were put down, he would take a bigger weapon and use it to get him deeper into the complex.

Hunt climbed out of the vehicle and kept his right hand on his pocket, the fingers wrapped around the butt of the handgun.

With Wang beside him, they walked up to the bunker entrance. The guards turned to meet their approach. All four were armed with QBZ-191s.

Hunt and Wang stepped up to the four guards and stopped. Hunt was about to draw his weapon when ten soldiers seemingly appeared from thin air.

Hunt looked confusedly at Wang.

"I was wondering when you would show," Mei Ling said.

"Well shit," Hunt hissed.

She wore her hair up un a tight bun and the uniform of a Chinese colonel. "I'm sorry for the deception but we had to be sure that we scooped up everyone."

"So, you're a double agent," Hunt said.

"No, I'm a member of the Chinese Communist Party Special Investigation Unit. Change is coming and so is the purge."

"Bitch," Wang snarled.

"Search them and take them away to be questioned. I will take care of it personally."

Hunt looked at Wang again and said, "That fucked that."

————

TAIPEI, TAIWAN

"The tunnel's blocked ahead," Norris said to Groves. "We'll have to backtrack to the last exit point."

"I thought everything was supposed to be clear?"

"It was, but I'd say there was a missile strike which has caused the collapse."

"Shit. All right, turn around. Let's get above ground."

It took twenty minutes to get back to the ladder which returned them to the surface and fresh air. Norris and Helen went up first, forming a small defensive area while the others came up.

The skyline held an orange hue from the fires burning across Taipei. Groves climbed out of the manhole and did a 360-degree turn. "This is far worse than anything we expected."

Once everyone was finally above ground, he gathered them around. "Helen, you're on point. Rose, can you get us an uplink with your computer?"

She shook her head. "I just tried, and we got nothing. It looks like the Chinese have shut down all communications."

"All right, this is what we'll do. We fly out of here."

A jet roared overhead.

"With those things flying around?" Cross asked.

"Rose, find me a plane."

Her fingers danced across the keyboard of the

Toughbook. "There is a small airport five klicks from our present position."

Groves looked at Nelson. "You think you can make it?"

He nodded. "I'll make it. But what do we do once we get airborne?"

"We go and find the sub."

"But how do we land out there?" Nelson asked.

"We don't. We crash. It should be fun, actually."

Nelson just stared at the ODIN commander. Norris said, "You know what? Sometimes I just think the boss is plain crazy."

Groves said, "Move."

They walked along the street in single file with Helen on point. In the distance, explosions and the rattle of gunfire could be heard. Jets crisscrossed the sky and traffic started to grow heavy as people fled the city. Suddenly the air seemed to be torn apart overhead.

"Get down!" Groves shouted as a building further along the street exploded outwards from a missile striking it.

The team plus one gathered themselves and hesitated, looking at the devastation and flames where the façade of the building had been. Figures began wandering out on the street in a daze. One of them started to walk past Helen in a dreamlike state. She noticed that it was a man, and most of the skin had been burned from his body.

Helen winced. "Fuck. We need to help them."

"No," Groves said. "Keep moving."

More people emerged onto the road. The ODIN team turned right at the end of the street and walked into a traffic jam. Not just that, the whole scene before them was one of chaos. Then came the shooters.

The street erupted in gunfire. People began to run, while others fell under the hail of bullets.

"Where are the shooters?" Norris shouted.

"I don't know," Helen called back.

Groves grabbed Rose by the shoulder. "Watch the president."

"Yes, sir."

"Follow me," the ODIN leader said.

Finally broke through, they saw them. Five shooters firing indiscriminately in all directions.

"We need to stop them," Groves shouted, bringing his weapon up.

The MP5 came to life and the Chinese shooter fell under the blows of the bullets to his chest. Beside Groves, Helen opened fire and a second sleeper went down.

"RPG!" Cross shouted, and they all went to ground.

The rocket propelled grenade streaked overhead and slammed into a building. Flame and debris erupted from the blast, showering the fleeing people.

"Crossy, get that prick," Norris growled.

Cross took aim and fired, and the RPG man died instantly.

One by one they picked off the shooters until the death of the penultimate one triggered another incident. The remaining sleeper started to run towards a large group of fleeing Taiwanese. Groves watched him, puzzled by his actions.

Then he disappeared in a burst of flame, smoke, blood, and guts. The suicide vest he wore not only ripped his body apart but those of everyone around him.

"Shit," Groves growled, ducking reflexively.

"Did you see that?" Cross snarled. "That prick just detonated a vest."

"We need to keep moving," Groves said. "Now."

———

HEREFORD, ENGLAND

The door to Hank Jones's office opened and his secretary walked in. Jones looked away from the television screen he'd been watching and turned it off."

"What news, Eileen?" he asked.

"I've heard from three of the strike teams, sir. Anaconda, Mamba, and Viper were all successful and will be returning in due course. Team Reaper will be touching down soon, and ODIN is still out of contact. As for Mister Hunt, I'm not sure."

"What about Strike Team Rattler?"

"They should be jumping soon."

Jones remained silent.

"You look worried, sir."

"I keep getting the feeling that Rattler is jumping into a volcano."

"They are good, sir. Larry Vines will see them through."

"I hope so, Eileen."

She hesitated.

"What is it?"

"Dick Thompson from Anaconda was killed in the operation, sir."

"Damn it. Were they wearing their suits?"

"Yes, sir," Eileen replied. "I think he was shot in the head."

"Thank you, Eileen. He had a family? Am I right?"

"Yes, sir, a younger brother. He wasn't married or anything."

"See that his death benefits go to his brother. And go home. It's eighteen hundred."

"Yes, sir."

She left the office and Jones picked up his phone. He dialed a number from memory and a voice answered, "West."

"Jeremy, Hank Jones."

"There's certainly a shit storm kicking up, Hank. What can I do for you?"

"Three of my strike teams have completed their missions, the fourth should be jumping into Mexico soon. I don't know what else is happening with the US President. We've lost contact with ODIN."

"We've picked up some chatter from Harding's people and it would seem that they were successful. After that everything went dark. All that can happen now is they reach the sub."

"Here's hoping."

"I must say that Team Reaper of yours, does good work."

"They're Mary's team, Jeremy. I just sit back and watch what they do."

"I heard they lost a man and ended with two more in the hospital."

"Yes. They fight hard and lose big when they do. This whole thing is just a massive shit show and we've lost comrades and friends. And we're not done yet."

"Sing out if you need any more help, Hank. Good luck."

"Thanks, Jeremy."

Jones hung up and picked up the remote again and turned the television back on. It was the same revolving shot over again. American planes taking off from the carrier, *Washington*. "This needs to end soon, before some prick hits the wrong button."

———

OVER WESTERN CHINA

The Co-32 bounced as it was hit by un updraft before settling down into a smooth flight once again. The team was now kitted up and ready for rapid deployment. Rosanna would remain on the plane when it took off. Swift tasked to join the others. All were armed with M6A2s and P226 handguns. Cara, however, carried a little more firepower than the others. She had an L129A1 rifle chambered for 7.62mm rounds with an optimum range of 1,000 meters.

Kane pressed the transmit button on his comms and said, "Comms check."

The rest of the team checked in without any issues. Then he sat next to Liu. "How are you doing, sir?"

Liu nodded. "I am fine."

"That's good."

"Do you think this will work?" the Chinese President asked.

"There's only one way to find out, sir. If we can get you on air talking to the people then yes, it just might work."

"But can you get me on air, as you say?" Liu asked.

"If anyone can, it'll be Slick," Kane said. "However, you must understand, if things go sideways, then there may be a shootout. I'll not let any of the PLA kill my people."

"I understand."

"I hope so, sir, because this is all about you stopping a war."

"What about President Nelson?" Liu asked.

"At the moment, as far as I know, he is being extracted from Taiwan so he can do the same thing. This only works if you both can accomplish what you're trying to do."

Liu had been monitoring things on an iPad. He held it up. "If I allow things to continue then eventually Taiwan will be back where it belongs."

"Yes, sir, but at what cost? A lot of people have already died. If this keeps up, the conflict will draw more countries into the war. North Korea is just waiting to see what happens. We've received reports that they have already deployed fifteen divisions along the DMZ. Russia has deployed twenty divisions ready to sweep east. NATO forces are moving to stand in their way. You see, sir? This is just the beginning. There are so many repercussions that can and will eventuate if this is allowed to continue."

"Ladies and gentlemen, we're two minutes from touchdown."

"Do not worry, Mister Kane, I will hold my end up, as you American's say."

"Thank you, sir."

They all strapped themselves in once more and before they knew it, the wheels of the modified

Concorde touched the runway and it rumbled along until the reverse thrust kicked in, slowing it dramatically. It turned at the end of the runway and powered down, disgorging its passengers apart from Rosanna.

Once they had moved away from the Co-32, Kane said into his comms, "Thanks for the ride, Eagle One. Good luck on the way home."

"Good luck to you, Reaper One. I have a feeling you'll need it."

Suddenly headlights were seen bouncing on the darkened horizon. "Time for you to go, Eagle One, we've got Tangos inbound."

Soon the pilot had the throttles pushed all the way forward, the plane shaking as it roared. Then it seemed to leap forward as the brakes were released and it rocketed along the rugged runway, lifting into the air like a giant bird.

Kane turned to the others. "We need to get under cover. Everyone make sure you have your NVGs on."

Cara was looking through the scope on her rifle. "Too late, Reaper. We've got company."

Then gunfire ripped through the night.

———

"Slick, keep the president alive," Kane snapped. "The rest of us will give you cover. Head north, there is some cover in the ravines."

Bullets cut through the night, every now and then a red tracer sliced its way through the darkness. The team split into two groups of two. Traynor and Arenas going left, while Kane and Cara went right. Ahead of them the pair of headlights grew to four, then six as the follow vehicles fanned out. Cara brought up her DMR and fired at the windscreen of the lead technical with the machinegun on the back.

She fired round after round at the approaching Chinese vehicle until it suddenly veered off course. The vehicle turned sharply and then flipped violently, rolling over. Cara grunted with satisfaction and switched her aim.

Meanwhile the rest of the team had opened fire. The second vehicle exploded in flames while the third slowed to a stop after the driver was hit and his foot slipped off the gas pedal.

"Push forward," Kane ordered.

The four team members moved towards the vehicles, firing as they went. Soon the incoming fire was silenced, and they stopped shooting. Kane said, "Check for wounded."

They found two wounded lying near the last vehicle. They patched them as best they could and left them where they lay. Kane gathered the rest of them around. "Carlos, see if that last vehicle still runs. If it does, we can use it."

Cara said, "There is no way of knowing if they got off a radio transmission or not. If they did, we're in the shit before we leave."

Kane nodded. "That's why we'll change our route of travel. Slick, find me something."

"Roger that."

"Let's do this."

SALTILLO, MEXICO

Larry Vines, commander of Strike Team Rattler, hated doing operations in the middle of the day, especially in the middle of hostile territory. It took away an element of cover that made him feel safer. Plus, it was too damn hot to be running surveillance in a shitting van.

Jim Duncan was sitting behind the wheel while Sam Thomas and Paul Simon were in the back as well.

"Boss, we need to do something in a hurry because we're attracting some attention about now," Duncan said. "I've got tattooed motherfuckers starting to get a neckache out the front here."

"Just stick with the plan, Jim," Vines replied. "We'll get ready to assault once we get confirmation."

"That's all well and good but these cartel pricks are starting to get fucking nervous."

"All we need is confirmation, Jim. That's all."

Team Rattler had dropped in from a C-17 outside of Saltillo where they met an MI6 agent who set them up with their ride. They had brought their own weapons, all M6A2s. From there they had driven into the city and taken up an OP waiting for confirmation that their targets were on site.

The intel was yet to come through, but attention was building.

"I've got a banger coming towards the van," Duncan said.

Vines noticed him reach for his P226. "Jim, take it easy."

"It would be fine except the prick has a Mac Ten."

"Let's just see what happens."

The cartel man came up to the window and tapped on it. "Put the window down."

"What?"

"Put the fucking window down."

Duncan wound it down. "What's the problem?" he asked.

"What are you doing here?"

"Not much."

"Answer the question, man."

"Mate, don't do this," Duncan warned him.

"Are you telling me what to do, motherfucker?"

"Walk away, my friend."

He started to bring the Mac-10 up. "You don't tell me—"

The P226 appeared in the window opening and it shattered the heat of the day. The banger's head snapped back and he fell to the hot asphalt on the street.

"Shit," growled Vines. "That's bloody torn it. We move now."

They pulled their masks down and tumbled from the van. The other cartel bangers were starting to act as well. Vines knew what was coming. A full-on shootout on the streets with psycho bastards.

The suppressed M6 carbines started their deadly work as bangers began to fall. Moments later an influx of shooters joined the fray and opened fire. Rattler were now under intense fire.

"This isn't good," Simon said as he reloaded behind the van. Bullets punched into it creating the sound of hail hammering a tin roof. After reloading, he leaned around the rear of the van and opened fire once again. "You need to make a decision, Larry!"

"Try to push forward."

Jim Duncan broke cover and tried to shoot his way forward. Dropping a cartel shooter, he then switched his aim to another. He stopped suddenly and stiffened, jerking twice more before he went down.

"Jim's down! Jim's down!" Thomas shouted above the gunfire.

"Can you get to him?" Vines called back.

"No, I'm pinned down."

"Simon, can you get—"

"*RPG!*"

The rocket propelled grenade reached out and touched the van a heavy blow. It was thrust to the side, hitting the men who sheltered behind it with tremendous force. Flames enveloped them, burning skin black like charcoal.

Vines lay on his back, listening to the piercing shrieks filling his ears. Then he realized it was him making the noise. A figure loomed over him, but he couldn't make out who it was. The smell of burned flesh hung thickly in the air

Larry Vines never heard the shot that killed him.

———

HEREFORD, ENGLAND

The phone on Hank Jones's desk rang four times before he reluctantly picked it up. He paused before saying, "Hank Jones."

"Sir, this is Martha Price from communications, call sign Juliet."

"Yes, Miss Price?"

"Sir—" She hesitated. "Sir we have a team down in the field. Strike Team Rattler is unresponsive, and we've lost communications."

"Since when, Miss Price?"

"Five minutes ago, sir."

"Can it just be a communications glitch?" Jones asked.

"No, sir."

"All right, Miss Price. This is what I want you to do. Notify the British Embassy in Mexico City and then MI6. Ask them nicely if they could send someone to check it out."

"Yes, sir."

"Do you have ISR of the area?"

"Yes, sir."

"Get me everything you can. And see how the HVTs act. If they run, I want to know where to."

"Yes, sir," Miss Price replied.

Jones disconnected and stared at the screen on the wall. "Can this day get any damn worse?"

CHAPTER 17

TAIPEI, TAIWAN

THE FIGHTING WAS SPREADING throughout the streets. It was like guerilla warfare except the guerillas had an army of 10,000 in the country already. And while the Taiwanese forces were trying to organize themselves, the enemy was running amok.

ODIN was still moving and taking fire. They had traveled a good distance but now they were pinned down once more by a handful of shooters who had set up a strongpoint on the rooftop of a two-story apartment building.

Three police vehicles burned on the street illuminating bodies lying next to them. Groves looked at Helen and Norris. "We need to clear that rooftop."

"We can go around," Helen told him.

"We could but leaving them there will only make it worse for the next poor sods who come along."

"All right, we'll do it," she said. "Chuck?"

"I'm in."

They broke away from the others who kept up some covering fire. The biggest problem the team was facing was the state of their ammunition. It was running low.

Smith reached the doorway and stepped under the small awning which reached out from the stucco wall. Norris joined her. He said, "You know this is a dumb idea, right?"

"Our job is to follow orders, Chuck, not question them."

"Yeah, right," he grunted and tried the door. It swung open and he said, "Ladies first."

"I'm not a bloody lady," she said and hustled through the opening.

They located the stairs and started up. The first floor was clear, so they started up to the second. The gunfire grew louder the higher they went. Over the comms, Groves said, "Any day now is good."

"Roger. We're on it."

When they reached the door, Helen tried the knob. It was locked so she raised her MP5 and shot it before kicking it open. Stepping through onto the rooftop, Helen sighted her weapon onto the nearest shooter, and dropped him with a short burst.

Behind her Norris moved away and forward to be clear of her when he opened fire. The MP5 rattled from another short burst and a second shooter dropped, falling forward off the building.

The remaining three shooters whirled around and opened fire. Helen and Norris ran for the cover of the air conditioning towers. Helen could hear them shouting out in their native tongue, giving each other directions. She leaned around the tower and opened fire at a shooter who was trying to flank them. The man staggered under the strike of the bullets. He stayed upright momentarily so she shot him again. This time he fell.

On the other side, another shooter was doing the same as he tried to flank them. Norris muttered, "No you don't, mate."

The MP5 sent a stream of bullets out which brought the shooter down on the run. He skidded on his face and never moved.

That left a final one but Helen was all over it. Sensing the threat, she whirled, falling backward, landing hard as the bullets from the Chinese sleeper cut through the air above her. She raised her weapon and squeezed the trigger.

Then there were none.

Norris pulled her to her feet. "I guess we won."

"Uh, huh. We need to get moving, we've got a sub to catch."

Back down on street level, Groves and the others were waiting. "That was good work."

"They were careless," Helen said. "They're more like untrained militia. Spray and pray."

Groves nodded and turned to Rose. "Rosey, how far to go?"

"Under a klick."

"Then let's move."

WESTERN CHINA

"There it is," Kane said as they stared at the Chinese

base before them. "Our target is the building with the large satellite dish on it."

"This might be a silly question, Mister Kane," Liu said. "But why don't we go down there and talk to the base commander."

"Do you know him personally?" Kane asked.

"No."

"Then there's a good chance we would be shot without so much as a question being asked. We get down there, take the building, get the transmission out, and go from there."

"This is sounding more and more like a one-way trip every time I hear it," Cara said.

Kane's expression turned grim. "There are a lot of people dying tonight. Let's make sure we're not one of them."

"Amigo," Arenas said, "it has been a nice life."

"It has, my friend."

"Right up until I met you. Then all you want to do is get me killed."

Kane slapped him on the back. "I'm trying pretty hard this time."

"Then let us see if you can succeed."

"Request permission to be reassigned," Traynor said, trying to present a serious face but failing.

"Denied."

He started forward. "In that case, I'll see you in hell."

"Race you," Kane said in a low voice.

The team moved down to the perimeter fence, stopping just long enough to break through. They waited until the perimeter guards passed by before slipping into the compound itself. There was a good 200 meters of open ground between the fence and the buildings. They traversed it slowly, the searchlights making them even more cautious.

Kane waited for another sweep then pointed at the communications building. "Cara, up top. I want you up there watching everything that happens. Carlos can go with you. We'll make the uplink and get the transmission out."

"Copy."

They moved again, this time as far as the buildings. A guard appeared, lazy, tired. Kane hit him from behind and dragged him into the shadows. They made their way between the buildings until they reached the one they wanted. Kane said to Brick, "You ready?"

"Let's do it."

They entered the building and immediately started to clear it. What they did was cold, calculated killing. There was no reason to take any chances. What they had to do meant saving the lives of thousands. Once it was cleared, Kane turned to Swift. "Get me that uplink now."

Cara and Arenas went to the rooftop. They took up position where they could see the approaches to the main building. Cara said into her coms, "Reaper One, Reapers Two and Three are in position. No sign of trouble as yet."

Kane acknowledged the transmission and then said into his own comms, "Bravo, copy?"

"Reaper One. This is Zero, read you loud and clear."

"Roger, Zero. We are on target attempting to make the uplink. So far so good."

"Copy, keep us updated. Out."

The computer tech's fingers danced across the keyboard. The screen was full of numerals and letters that Kane didn't understand. The code seemed to roll down the screen. Swift turned to look at Kane and said, "I need a camera. Find me a camera somewhere."

Kane looked around and then found a Nikon. He held it up. "Will this do?"

Swift nodded. "I can make it work."

A few minutes later, Swift got up from his chair, searching for something to put the camera on, then linking it into the computer. "I'm almost ready."

Kane looked at the president. "Are you ready, sir?"

"I think so."

"Slick, are you sure you can override the blocking system they have in place?"

"Fingers are gold, my friend, fingers are gold."

"Shit," Kane said shaking his head.

"Reaper One. Do you copy?" Cara asked.

"Copy, Reaper Two. What's the problem?"

"I have a roving patrol heading our way. Requesting instructions."

"Shoot only if you have to, Reaper Two."

"Roger that."

"Slick, where are we at?"

"Good to go."

Kane turned to Liu. "Sir, take a seat."

Two minutes later, the Chinese president was broadcasting to his country. Three minutes after that, Cara opened fire. A minute after that, the signal was jammed.

———

One of the hangars was on fire and there were craters across the field. Groves said, "It looks like the air strip was hit by rockets."

"That's not all," said Helen. "I've got X-rays everywhere."

"Can you see a plane?"

"Nothing intact, so far. It looks like they were all taken out—wait, I might have something."

"A plane?" asked Groves.

"Yes, looks like an old Douglas DC3."

"Great," Norris hissed. "A fucking relic."

"Can you fly it, Paul?" Groves asked.

"If it has wings, sir, I can get it up."

"Rose, any luck on raising the sub?"

Rose shook her head. "Nothing. Once we get airborne and out over the ocean, I might have better luck."

"Copy. All right, let's steal a plane. Helen, cover our flank."

Helen dropped the backpack she was carrying and opened it up. She proceeded to withdraw metal pieces and put them together. Soon she had assembled an Accuracy International AWM sniper rifle chambered for .338.

"Ready when you are," she said.

They started across the airfield, Helen walking off to the side, sweeping, searching. She suddenly stopped and fired. In the fire glow near a burning plane, an armed man fell.

Helen kept going, sweeping again. Cross brought

up the rear. She heard his MP5 fire briefly followed by a grunt of satisfaction.

In the center of the column, Nelson kept up with Rose who watched her side with only a handgun. Ahead of them the DC3 grew larger. So did the armed men around it. One of them turned and called out. Norris opened fire with the MP5SD he carried.

The armed man had been trying to bring his weapon to bear but never made it. However, the others did and opened fire.

Bullets ripped through the air. Rose pushed Nelson to the ground and knelt over him. It took most of the magazine from her handgun before a shooter fell.

The firing intensified but again, the shooters were poor shots. They were getting closer, but before they could zero in, the highly trained ODIN team had them down.

"X-rays down, push to the plane," Groves said.

Rose dragged Nelson to his feet and shoved him forward. "Keep going, mate, not long now."

"Thank God for that."

"Just remember to hold to your end of the deal."

"I will."

They reached the DC3 and checked the door. It was open so while Cross climbed in to check it out, the others formed a perimeter. Except for Nelson who was unceremoniously shoved inside.

In the cockpit, Cross checked everything then tried the starboard motor. It fired to life. He pumped his fist and then tried the port one. Again, it roared to life. He pulled back the window to the side and called out, "Everyone get on board. ODIN Airlines is now leaving."

The team climbed aboard the DC3, Groves into the copilot seat. "How much fuel?"

Cross looked at the gauge. "We should have enough."

Helen poked her head through the cockpit door opening. "Better get this thing in the air, we've got a vehicle approaching. From the other side of the airfield."

The sound of bullets hammering into the plane reached their ears. "Check that," Helen said, "they're already hear."

"Keep them off us," Cross said as the plane started to taxi. "I need a few more minutes."

Cross turned the DC3 onto the taxiway, all too aware of the incoming gunfire. All it would take was a bullet in the wrong place and it would be all for nothing.

The plane bumped along, and a bullet ricocheted off the window near Cross's head. "Great, come this far to get shot down before we even take off."

"Maybe get us in the air so we can be shot down," Groves suggested helpfully with a shrug.

"Yeah, right."

When the taxiway met the main runway, Cross turned the plane left. He said, "Short takeoff."

"Are you sure you can get it up?"

"I guess we'll find out, otherwise we risk getting the shit shot out of us and we'll never get the bitch up."

He pushed the throttles all the way forward and the plane started to shake. The motors roared and he could feel the winged beast wanting to go. Cross released the brakes and the plane started to rumble forward.

Bullets still hammered the thin skin of the DC3,

punching through. Groves glanced at Cross who was mumbling to himself.

The ODIN commander looked out through the window in front and saw the end of the runway approaching fast. "Are you going to take off soon?"

"Almost there, Boss," Cross replied.

The white stripes at the end of the runway slid beneath the nose.

"Now is good, Crossy."

"Almost—there."

Then came the grass off the end followed by the fence. Groves closed his eyes and muttered, "Fuck me."

Groves closed his eyes and waited for the crunch. But it never came. When he opened his eyes he saw that the nose of the DC3 was rising. He looked at Cross and could see a more relaxed expression on his team member's face. Groves said, "I gather we're not going to die?"

"We haven't put her down yet, boss."

"Don't I know it. Point us towards the sub, Paul. We're racing the clock."

———

WESTERN CHINA

"Damn it, Slick, get it back up, now," Kane rumbled. "We need to get that transmission out."

"I'm working on it, Reaper," Swift said, concentrating on his keyboard.

"Cara, talk to me."

"We're...heavy..."

"Say again."

"We're taking heavy fire, Reaper. The Chinese forces are building up rather quickly."

Kane looked at Traynor. "Go and give them a hand."

"Roger that."

"I've got it," Swift blurted out. "We're back up."

"Get transmitting. Mister President, here we go again."

CHAPTER 18

ODIN

ROSE STUCK her head into the cockpit and said, "I've made contact with the sub."

"Good lass," Groves said. "Where are they?"

"Right where we asked them to be." She looked out the window and realized just how low they were over the ocean. "Holy shit."

Cross chuckled. "Did you bring your fishing pole, Rosey?"

"I hate fishing."

"I hope you like swimming because in—" the DC3 bounced from turbulence, "in a few minutes we're ditching. You'd better get everyone strapped in."

"Great, I hope there aren't any sharks."

"Can you patch me through to the sub?"

"Consider it done."

A few moments later, Cross said, "Barracuda this is Odin, over."

Nothing.

He tried again. "Barracuda, this is Odin, over."

"Receiving you, Odin."

"We're coming up on your position."

"We haven't picked you up on sonar, Odin."

"That's because we're coming in by air, Barracuda," Cross explained.

"Then how—oh."

"We'll be down in a couple of minutes."

"Good luck. We're surfacing now. Will illuminate so you have something to home in on. Best of British, old chap."

Cross circled until the sub came to the surface and a light came on. "Got it," he said, pointing to his ten o'clock. "This is it. I'll try to bring it down close. Get ready."

Cross straightened the DC3 and brought it in parallel to the sub. He dropped the revs on the motors and lost what little height he had.

Then just before it touched the water, he pulled the throttles back until the plane had lost all power. Then it dropped.

———

"Everyone out," Groves called as the plane started to settle in the water. "Open the escape hatch over the wing. Then jump into the water. Leave all your gear."

Norris cracked the hatch and pointed out into the darkness, nodding at Helen. "Ladies first."

"Shark bait don't you mean?" she shot back at him, stripping down to her underwear.

Her comrade said, "You been working out?"

"Get your gear off."

"I'll chance it."

"No underwear, huh?"

"Not a fucking bit."

"Idiot."

Soon they were all undressed and one by one getting out onto the wing. From there they jumped into the rolling sea. True to her tasking, Rose watched over Nelson. "That wasn't too bad," he said as he bobbed up and down.

"As long as the sharks don't get us," she replied.

"There are sharks here?" His head pivoted quickly on his neck, looking in all directions.

As Cross swam past, he said, "Yeah, big fat mother-fuckers who like to eat politicians."

Suddenly a light appeared sweeping the ocean's surface, then a dinghy with three sailors in it. "Are you alright?"

"Yes," Groves called back.

"Good to hear. Let's get you aboard so you can complete your mission."

"Do you have a secure uplink?"

"Yes."

"Then let's do it," Groves said. *Mission complete.*

WASHINGTON DC

All eyes watched the screens as President Nelson spoke, ordering the American forces to stand down. He then started to outline what was happening and how at that same moment, the President of China was ordering his own forces to do the same thing. Coster turned to the man beside him. "Is it true?"

"Partly, sir. The Chinese air force has turned around and are ceasing operations over Taiwan. The ground forces will take a little more. We're unsure about their naval forces." The man's cell buzzed. He checked it. "Sir, the joint chiefs have just ordered a cessation of all hostilities and the Justice Department have issued a warrant for your arrest. It would be prudent for you to leave."

"Damn it, what went wrong?"

"I don't know, sir." Hesitation. "Sir, we need to go."

Coster nodded. "Yes, we do."

TEAM REAPER

Cara sighted on her next target and squeezed the trigger. The L129A1 slammed back into her shoulder and the Chinese soldier dropped. Five more took his place. They were running low on ammunition and all of them were wounded in some way. Luckily they wore their Synoprathetic suits. Beside her, Arenas grunted and doubled over.

"That is the second time," he groaned.

Traynor slapped his friend on the back and said, "Try being shot three times. It hurts worse."

"Screw you."

"Oh, shit," Cara snapped, seemingly stunned. "Reaper, we've got a tank."

"A what?"

"A frigging Type 99 tank."

BOOM!

The tank rocked and the shell roared over the building like a freight train. The three Team Reaper operators ducked reflexively.

Cara jumped to her feet. "Time to—"

The tank fired again, this time hitting the upper part of the dish, shredding it. "There goes the transmission," Traynor said.

Cara looked out at the tank and saw the turret traversing. "Mother—"

The rest was drowned out as the tank exploded in fire. "What was that?" Traynor asked.

Suddenly a giant jet-propelled bird flew low overhead with a deafening roar. As Cara looked up, she saw the Co-32 disappearing into the distance. "You didn't think we were going to leave you hanging out to dry on your own, did you?" a familiar voice asked.

"Really glad to see you, Eagle One," Cara said.

Kane appeared on the rooftop with Liu. The Chinese President had a megaphone in his hand. Cara frowned. "What are you doing?"

"The message got out. Now we have to stop this. Liu says he can get through to them."

"Well don't let him stand up or it'll be over before he begins."

Kane turned to Liu. "It's all yours."

It took two minutes of talking before the state of things began to alter. The firing died away and the Chinese PLA soldiers walked out into the open. Liu stood up and his words became higher-pitched, and to the soldiers before him, mesmerizing. Kane looked at Cara. "I think we've done it."

She nodded, relief etched in her face. "I think you're right."

———

BORDEN HUNT

The door to the cell opened and Mei Ling walked in, her high heels clunking on the concrete floor. In her hand was the bomb in the case. Hunt stared at her. "What do you want?"

"Listen, we don't have much time if this is going to work."

Hunt glanced at Wang. "What is happening?"

Wang said, "Mei Ling is who she says she is and has been investigating Sun for the past two years. This is the culmination of that investigation. Arresting us was the only way of getting in."

"Why didn't you say something?" Hunt asked.

"We couldn't," Mei Ling replied. "But enough for now. We have to take care of Sun. your friends have succeeded in rescuing the president. But Sun has an ace up his sleeve. He is planning to send launch codes to our submarines to launch tactical nuclear weapons on Taiwan. If he succeeds, there will be no coming back."

"Then we'd better stop him."

"Follow me," Mei Ling said.

She opened the door and revealed a soldier standing outside. He looked at her and said, "Well, Colonel?"

"We do it now, Captain."

"Fine." He looked at Hunt and handed him a suppressed handgun. "You will need this."

Mei Ling turned to face Wang. She handed him the

case with the bomb inside. "Count to twenty and then follow us to the bunker. We will clear a path for you. If we do not make it, then it is up to you."

Wang nodded.

Mei Ling looked at Hunt. "This is it."

———

Wang did as he was ordered. He counted and then moved. Somewhere ahead of him in the winding hallway, he could hear numerous gunshots. As he rounded a corner, he found the first body. That of a plain-clothes operative, more likely from the Ministry of State Security. His blood had pooled on the concrete around his head, his handgun lay beside him. Wang scooped it up and kept walking.

Around the next corner he found two men dressed in uniform. Both dead. One was a major, the other was the captain who had been with Mei Ling. He'd been shot in the chest and head, his eyes still open, sightless.

Wang continued walking. Now the alarm was wailing and a voice sounding over the speakers on the walls.

The next corner revealed four soldiers, all leaking blood onto the hard floor. Three were dead, the fourth, was alive, propped up against the wall, a bloody hand pressing against a wound in her side. Mei Ling looked up at him. "K—keep going."

"Are you dying?" Wang asked.

"No, I do not think so."

He leaned down and grabbed her arm. "Then get up, Colonel. There is still work to be done."

Mei Ling cried out in pain as he dragged her to her

feet. Wang leaned down, picked up a weapon, and thrust it into her hand. "Now move."

The gunfire was louder now, it sounded as though Hunt was making a good fist of it. There were two more turns to go and then they would reach the bunker. Around the first of those turns, there was another soldier dead on the concrete floor. Around the second, they found four more. Laid out before their killer who was down on his knees.

Hunt looked back over his shoulder at the two approaching figures. His face was a mask of pain. "I almost made it."

Mei Ling knelt beside him. He'd been shot three times. Once in the arm, twice in the torso. He was losing a good amount of blood. "Sorry," he apologized.

Wang looked down at him. "I will take it from here, Mister Hunt. It has been an honor."

Wang walked up to the steel blast door which led into the bunker. He tried his key card, but nothing happened. Then he opened the keypad and put in an override code which very few knew about. The door slid open, and he walked inside, letting it close behind him.

Hunt looked at Mei Ling. "What is he..."

The sound of the blast was blocked by the blast door, but it was faint. Mei Ling wrapped her arm around Hunt and said, "It is done. Now it will all stop."

Hunt gave her a weak smile.

"I hope so," he said and rolled slowly onto his side. He stared at the roof above him and then his eyes closed.

CHAPTER 19

HEREFORD, ENGLAND—ONE WEEK LATER

"YOU NEED to get me out of this room," Knocker moaned. "The bastard snores like a bloody chainsaw."

Brick waved a hand at his friend. "Whatever, I can't hear anything."

"That's because you're bloody asleep, mate. Christ, it's enough to suck the covers off my bed."

"I'm glad to see that you both are feeling better today," Rosanna Morales said to pair.

"I'm ready to go operational, Doc," Knocker urged her.

"Two weeks, Raymond," she replied with a knowing smile.

He screwed his face up. "Don't you go calling me Raymond. I get enough of that from the boss."

"Enough of what?" Mary Thurston asked as she walked into the hospital room.

"Oh, God, here she is."

"Do you have an issue, Raymond?"

Knocker looked at Rosanna. "See what I mean?"

She grinned at him. "I was just telling Mister Jensen that he will be in hospital for at least another two weeks."

"Hold up, you said operational."

"Just do what the Doc says, Knocker," Brick prodded him. "You know you will anyway."

"It will be an additional two weeks before you are operational."

"Shit a bloody brick."

"If you want something to do, Raymond," Thurston said, "I'm sure we can find you something. Instructing new recruits, maybe."

"I'd rather dip my eye in hot bird shit." Knocker paused. "How is Borden Hunt?"

It was Rosanna who answered. "He is still in an induced coma. We will wake him up in a couple of days."

"Is he going to be all right?"

"The signs are promising but we won't know until he is awake."

Knocker shook his head. "We certainly took a hit on this one. The admiral, Rucker, Anvil, Striker, Ruggles. A whole Strike team and a commander, and..."

Thurston nodded. "Yes, and Axel."

"What is this Odin team I've been hearing about?" Brick asked, changing the subject.

"They are Global's extraction team. Anything, anyone, anywhere. They are all Brits. Crashed a plane into the ocean next to a sub to deliver President Nelson."

"Crazy bastards," Brick said shaking his head. "Sounds like something Knocker would do."

"It worked. Things in Taiwan are quietening down and China and the US are at the UN discussing how to make things better."

"What about Nelson?" Brick asked.

"The bounty has been lifted and he is resigning before the enquiry comes around."

"And that prick, Coster?" Knocker asked.

"We might just have a lead there."

———

INDONESIAN ARCHIPELAGO—TWO WEEKS LATER

It was nighttime when the four swimmers came out of the water and walked up the white sands of the secluded island, dumping their kit at the edge of the jungle, to change. Moments later they were ready to move, NVGs pulled down and weapons up. They were going in with their suppressed M6A2s. No sniper system this time around; this was a capture mission. Their target was Randall Coster who was surrounded by Trent Forest and his shooters.

"Zero, copy?" Kane said into his comms.

"Read you loud and clear, Reaper One."

"We're feet dry and moving to the first checkpoint."

"Copy. Bravo One has an MQ-9 overhead with a full package should you need it."

"Roger that. Reaper One, out."

"Cara, you're on point. Carlos, on our six. We've got six hours to make the target. That'll give us two hours of dark left to complete the mission. Move out."

The intel about Coster had come from the Israelis. They had been running an op in Thailand which included surveillance of a terrorist who had been trying to acquire a WMD. It just so happened that Coster had popped up on their surveillance footage in the background.

Global had run their own surveillance operation using Jack Harris's Mamba. Hank Jones had tossed up whether to use Mamba for the extraction but decided against it, pulling them out the night before. Then there was ODIN, but they were already deployed on a different operation in France.

No, it would be better if Reaper were the ones who did it, after all they had already lost so much. A week before being deployed they had buried Axe. It had rained; hell, it always seemed to rain when someone was buried in the UK.

It had been a somber graveside service. Axe had no family after his sister had died. Only Reaper. They were his family. But others had come to bid farewell to the big former Marine. The Team from Talon, for one, ODIN for another. Hank Jones stood beside the heads of MI6 and MI5. They had been there because of their recognition of what Reaper had done for their country. Also the director of the CIA, a man named Bradley Franks. After the service he'd passed on the message that if the team wished to return to the US, they would be welcome. Mary Thurston hadn't even hesitated in telling him, no.

Kane had stood under an umbrella with his sister Melanie. He'd watched in silence as they lowered the big man's coffin into the English soil.

Later, the team all went to the pub to drown their sorrows, joined by the wheelchair-bound Knocker and Brick. The mood somehow developed after a couple of hours into wheelchair races in the parking lot. It was something that Axe would have enjoyed and been in the midst of if he'd been there.

Later that night, Cara and Kane lay beside each other in their bed. She had rolled over and said, "I don't know if I can do this anymore, Reaper."

Kane had nodded and replied, "I know what you mean."

———

They walked through the jungle dripping with moisture from the afternoon storms. The air was humid, and the night life was out in force. They traversed ravines and steep ridges. Creeks and muddy slopes. Insects were nasty, and snakes were present. Cara paused as she topped the last ridge. She crouched down and stared at the lights in the distance.

Kane moved up beside her and said, "Is that it?"

"I hope so, I'm sick of climbing ridges."

"Take us in."

An hour later they reached the perimeter. It wasn't fenced; there was no need. No one expected anyone to come at the compound from across the ridges through the jungle. Not when the place had its own private beach.

"Bravo One, copy?" Cara asked over her comms.

"Copy, Reaper Two."

"We're on target. Need a real time update."

"You have four guards as a roving patrol, three more within the grounds. We're also reading heat signatures inside the main building. All are unmoving."

"Copy. We're moving in."

The last thing Cara thought before she started the assault was, *I hope we don't fuck this up.*

––––––

Famous last words.

The team had split and set off motion sensors. Soon an alarm was going off and a firefight had broken out. The whole yard lit up and flared the team's NVGs. Kane had ordered the power cut which Traynor and Arenas had accomplished. Then in the dark once more, the advantage turned in the favor of the assaulters.

However, Trent Forest and his team were hardened veterans and weren't about to give in too easy. The battle grew fiercer, but Team Reaper were up to the fight. There was vengeance to extract.

Kane had called in an air strike from the UAV. Two Hellfires had been loosed with devastating effect.

The massive blasts set the defenders back on their heels long enough for Reaper to enter the house.

The team dropped two shooters in the entry way before once more dividing. Arenas and Traynor went upstairs to clear while Kane and Cara worked the lower level.

They made their way towards the kitchen and ran into two more shooters. One of which they recognized immediately. Trent Forest.

"I see you're still alive, Kane," he called out in between bursts of fire. "Couldn't you do us all a favor and just die?"

"Not today, Forest."

More gunfire ripped through the air above Kane's head. Cara fired a long burst before reloading the M6 with a fresh magazine. Kane fired a burst and regained cover. He lay his carbine down beside him and took out his P226. Cara frowned and asked, "What stupidity are you about to do?"

"Throw out a stun grenade."

"Reaper, this is a bad idea."

"Just do it, Cara. It ends here and now."

She unhooked a stun grenade from her webbing and pulled the pin. Then she threw it deep into the kitchen.

As soon as it blew, Kane was up and moving. The first person he saw was the man with Forest. Kane fired twice, making him stagger. Then Kane adjusted his aim and shot him in the head.

He switched his aim for Forest and was a fraction too slow. Maybe he should have looked for the mercenary first, for Forest was used to combat and had recovered almost immediately. He fired and Kane grunted, dropping to his knees.

"Reaper!" Cara shouted upon seeing him fall.

The Synoprathetic suit had taken the bullet, stopping it. The blow, however, had also stopped its wearer. Forest stepped forward, raising his weapon for an execution.

"No!" shouted Cara as she stepped out into the open. She dropped her M6 letting it hang by its strap, drawing the P226 in a fluid motion.

The weapon snapped into line with her target and Cara fired.

Once...twice...three times.

The rounds punched into Trent, his body jerking under each blow. He went to his knees, his gun dropping from his grasp. Keeping her P226 trained on him,

Cara walked forward. He looked up at her, blood running from the corner of his mouth. He gave her a wry grin. "Shit, killed by a bitch."

She raised her weapon again and shot him in the head.

"Reaper, are you alright?"

"Christ, that hurts," Kane said. "Help me up. We have to secure the rest of the building."

Meanwhile, upstairs, Arenas and Traynor were going room to room. As per usual, it was always the last room to be cleared, just like the movies, that they found their target.

Arenas breached and shot Coster's bodyguard before he could get off a shot. The man dropped next to Coster who was stunned by the sudden death of his man.

The former Mexican Special forces officer zip-tied Coster's hands behind his back and whispered into his ear, "We would like to kill you, Amigo, but we can't. So, a deep dark hole will be the place for you. Move."

Leading him from his room, they took him downstairs where Kane and Cara waited. Kane looked at the man and nodded with satisfaction. "Reaper One to Zero. We have the package and are ready for extraction."

"Copy, Reaper One. Good job."

———

HEREFORD, ENGLAND—THREE DAYS LATER

There were five beers, and four people seated around the table in the pub. Knocker and Brick were out of the hospital and still completing their rehab. They were there for two reasons. To celebrate the life of a fallen friend and for Kane and Cara to share some news with them.

It was Knocker who picked up on the vibe first. "All right, what is it?"

It was Cara who spoke first. "I'm being reassigned for a while."

The Brit stared at her incredulously. "What?"

"I requested it. I'm going to team training."

Knocker nodded. He understood. The last op had been a tough one. "Burn out is a bitch."

Cara nodded. "Yes."

"That's not all," Kane said. "All of us are being stood down and reassigned."

"Bullshit," Brick growled.

"Who the fuck is going to take over from us?" Knocker asked.

"They're going to assign one of the Strike Teams."

"How long for?"

Kane shrugged. "I don't know."

"Could it be permanent?"

"I don't know."

"Then what happens to us all?"

"Brick is going to train combat medics, and you are going to run support ops for Odin."

"A frigging desk job?"

"You could see it that way. But you know ops, and what you take to them could prove invaluable."

"What about you, Reaper?" Brick asked.

"I'm moving up to Zero-Two."

"Taking Carlos's job?" Knocker asked. "What about him?"

"He's moving over to the strike teams and taking over planning."

"Shit, this is a big shake up."

Cara nodded. "That isn't all. Brooke is leaving. She has had a job offer in Germany. She's decided to take it."

Knocker held up his beer. "So, Team Reaper is no more."

"For the moment," Kane replied. "But we'll be back."

The Brit nodded. "We always are."

Cara tapped her beer to Knocker's. "Old and absent friends."

"Old and absent friends," they all replied.

CHAPTER 20

"FALCON ONE-ZERO, TO BRAVO ZERO-TWO, OVER."

"Zero-Two reads you Lima Charlie, Falcon, over," Kane replied from the ops room in Gaborone, Botswana.

"We're two mikes from the LZ, over."

"Copy."

Onboard the helicopter known as Falcon One-Zero was Strike Team Hyena, led by Ollie Richards. They were a four-man team now operating under the purview of Team Reaper. They were in Botswana trying to root out poachers who had stepped up their activity against a small and diminishing herd of elephants in Chobe National Park.

The rangers had reached out for help after one of their anti-poaching teams was massacred by the poachers responsible. But on further investigation, the poachers were discovered to be more than a little hi-tech.

Global received the call and they dispatched their team. Their new team.

Swift had picked up chatter that a team of poachers were working in the park that night and Hyena, along with a team from the anti-poaching squad had been dispatched to intercept them. Now they were only a couple of minutes out from their designated landing zone.

"Talk to me," Thurston said from behind Kane and Ferrero.

The former DEA agent said, "Hyena is two mikes out and on time. Bravo One, how are we looking on the LZ?"

"LZ looks clear, no heat signatures at this time," replied a female voice.

It was still hard to get used to not having Brooke in the flying seat. The new Bravo One was Rani Perera, a Brit by birth from Sri Lankan parents. Before coming to Global she had flown Apache helicopters before crossing over to UAVs.

"*Falcon One-Zero is one mike out.*"

Kane said, "Do another sweep, make sure, Rani."

"Roger, coming around for another sweep."

"What about the elephant herd?" Thurston asked.

"One klick to the east," Swift replied. "The satellite shows them bunched near a waterhole."

"No other heat signatures?"

"No, ma'am."

Kane suddenly felt nervous. Everything was going so smooth. Too smooth. Beside him, Ferrero said,

"Relax, Reaper, they'll be on the ground in thirty seconds."

"Falcon One-Zero, flaring for landing."

"Oh, shit. Abort! Abort!" cried Rani. "Get out, now."

Suddenly the big screen came alive with heat signatures.

"What the hell?" Kane snapped. "Were they using some kind of cloaking material?"

In the background Ferrero was talking on the radio. "Falcon One-Zero, abort. I say again, abort. The LZ is hot."

"Roger, Falcon One-Zero is aborting—oh, shit!"

On the big screen back in ops, the Bravo team watched on in disbelief as an explosion ripped through the helicopter. The comms went dead and what remained of the craft crashed onto the ground. "Was that a missile or an RPG?" Kane barked.

No one answered.

"Missile or RPG?" he asked again, his voice harsher.

"Not sure at this time," Rani answered.

They all watched on as the heat signatures closed on the crash site.

Kane said, "Falcon One-Zero, copy?"

Static.

"Hyena One, copy?"

Static.

"Hyena Two, copy?"

Static.

"Hyena Three, copy?"

"They are all dead, American," an accented voice came back to ops. "Let this be a lesson to you. Stay out of Botswana. You do not belong here."

The line went dead.

Kane turned and stared at Ferrero. The former DEA man nodded. "All right, Reaper. Make some calls and get them together."

TEAM REAPER PAYS THE ULTIMATE PRICE DURING A FUTURE WAR ON DRUGS.

In the year 2030, the war on drugs has evolved into a brutal battle. Once-ordinary cartels have transformed into formidable forces, equipped with their own armies boasting tanks, jets, and submarines. And as the line between good and evil blurs, both sides are set to deploy cutting-edge weaponry in a deadly dance for control.

Enter Team Reaper. With a high-stakes battleground, where survival is measured in firepower and strategy, one highly-skilled unit—comprised of John Kane, Cara Billings, and Raymond "Knocker" Jensen—find themselves at the heart of the chaos, desperately trying to stem the growing tide of death known as Happy Days.

But as they navigate perilous landscapes and shifting alliances, the true cost of their actions becomes unclear. How much is too much when dealing in death is a daily routine?

Join Team Reaper as they confront the ultimate test of their convictions in a world of chaos. For some, it may just be their last fight.

AVAILABLE NOW